Also recommended...

You may also enjoy these other Forbidden Fiction works:

Blindsided by Ann Ruby
It begins as a case of mistaken identity. Brenda is escaping into the mountains of Montana for a week of relaxation. Instead, she finds herself naked and pressed against a hard, aroused man, intent on a weekend of sexual domination. When the real submissive walks in on them, he realizes the mistake made at the front desk and is horrified, willing to do whatever he can to make things right. Brenda is intrigued. When she asks him to take her on as a substitute, he is blindsided! Can a weekend that satisfies their deepest desires, both sexually and emotionally, turn into more? (M/F)
http://forbidden-fiction.com/library/story/AR1-1.000009

Deep Focus by M. L. Caufax
Zöe is nervous and excited to begin her first year at the exclusive university tucked away in a tiny forest town. Her new boss, Dean, is a handsome older man with captivating blue eyes, and an understanding smile. At Dean's suggestion, it seems only natural that Zöe should submit to her classmate Trevor's commanding advances when he comes to Dean for grief counseling after a bad breakup. Why shouldn't they put on erotic plays for Counselor Dean whenever he pleases? Only when Zöe is gifted with an ancient talisman that protects her from Dean's hypnotic gaze does she finally discover the horrible truth... (M/F, M/F/M)
http://forbidden-fiction.com/library/story/MLC-1.000124

Slowly blue eyes met his own,

shame evident in them, her face filled with consternation.

"Why does it bother you to tell me that?" he asked. "Just because he wasn't any of those things doesn't mean he wasn't a kidnapper. A rapist. He held you against your will and used you without permission. That isn't your fault. None of it was your fault."

"I know," she agreed readily. Too readily. "That's what my other therapists told me."

"But you don't believe them. Is that why you came to me?"

"No, I believe them," she rushed to say, again too quickly. Saying what she thought he wanted to hear. What she had been convinced was the right thing to say under the circumstances, but her flickering gaze revealed the lie for what it was.

"I don't believe you," he stated, releasing her hands and sitting back in the booth.

Covert Passion

Ann Ruby

ForbiddenFiction
www.forbiddenfiction.com

an imprint of

Fantastic Fiction Publishing
www.fantasticfictionpublishing.com

COVERT PASSION
A Forbidden Fiction book

Fantastic Fiction Publishing
Hayward, California

© Ann Ruby, 2014

CREDITS
Editors: Rylan Hunter, Elizabeth A. Tanner
Cover Design: D.M. Atkins
Cover Photos/Art: Photos by Chepko at Dreamstime. Additional design work by Siolnatine
Production Editor: Erika L Firanc
Proofreading: Jae Knight

SKU: AR1-000153-01 FFP
ISBN: 978-1-62234-168-9

Published in the United States of America

DISCLAIMER

This book is a work of fiction which contains explicit erotic content; it is intended for mature readers. Do not read this if it's not legal for you.

All the characters, locations and events herein are fictional. While elements of existing locations or historical characters or events may be used fictitiously, any resemblance to actual people, places or events is coincidental.

This story is not intended to be used as an instruction manual. It may contain descriptions of erotic acts that are immoral, illegal, or unsafe. Do not take the events in this story as proof of the plausibility or safety of any particular practice.

This work is dedicated to Farran, my editor in the making, and to Ruth, who has finally discovered pleasure reading vs. reading for pleasure.
Special thanks to my publisher D.M. Atkins and my editor Rylan Hunter, for seeing possibility where others have not.

Contents

Chapter 1

The Counselor

They say a man never forgets his first, but Devlin O'Malley had been trying to do just that for the last thirteen years. It was a quest that drove his every decision, determined the very direction of his life. There were times when it almost made him crazy, especially on nights like this. Whenever a cold March rain mixed with the air from the Atlantic to blanket the city in fog, he remembered that spring that changed his life.

Standing at his office window, forearm resting above his head on the glass pane, he stared with soulless eyes at the lights of Boston, muted by the weather, and listened to the couple dressing in the therapy room behind him. Forced himself to concentrate on the here and now. Took note of the sound of their voices, hushed, intimate, the rustle of their clothing, the unhurried nature of their movements.

The sexual surrogate had left a few minutes ago, giving him a quick verbal report that would be followed by a written summary tomorrow, but everything had gone well. Devlin was not surprised. He was relieved, though. Using a surrogate was something that many sex therapists shied away from and some considered to be borderline illegal, but in this case he thought it was the best treatment for the couple in the other room. They had an established and solid relationship, having been married for more than thirty years, and the danger of either one of them falling in love with a surrogate was almost non-existent.

When he had first suggested it to them, he was uncertain how they would react. Both had been raised in strict Irish Catholic households. Although that was part of what brought them to him in the first place, a lot of people like them would have run screaming. Most men would have taken the suggestion as a direct attack on their masculinity. Not George. He had listened to Devlin's explanation of why he thought a surrogate could help them, had conferred privately with his wife, and at their next appointment announced that they were willing to give it a try. George only wanted to make Mary happy.

According to the surrogate, it had worked. Both husband and wife were satisfied with the outcome of this night's session, with his services in general, and Devlin knew that they were no longer going to need him.

He was proved right a few minutes later when the woman said, "Mr. O?" and he turned to see her stepping into the office with her husband, both fully clad and wearing their jackets. Mary's cheeks were a little rosier than usual and George unnecessarily adjusted his collar, but they didn't avoid making eye contact with him.

"Yes, Mary?" he asked.

"We really want to thank you for everything you've done for us."

"My pleasure," he replied sincerely. He had enjoyed helping the two of them. They were the kind of people he wished he had been born to. George was an honest, hard-working man who owned his own swordfish boat and wore the effects of years at sea on his face. His blue eyes, surrounded by sun-baked wrinkles, had a permanent squint while his cheeks were as florid as any drunk even though he had given up liquor on his wedding day because his bride asked him to. He was big, and burly, and still adored the woman at his side after all this time, and no one who knew her could blame him. Where George was rough, Mary was diplomatic. Where he was often in a hurry and determined to wrap things up, Mary was patient and accepting; of people, of their differences, of the variations in their speeds and timetables.

"But we think we can take it from here on our own," she said now, and although she was speaking to Devlin, she looked up to her husband for reassurance. Her dark eyes were bright and soft, like that of the kindergarten children she taught during the day. George nodded and she turned back to Devlin.

This was always the awkward part for the client. People didn't know how to end a relationship with their sex therapist, especially when that therapy involved hands-on work, and especially if he worked with them as a couple, privy to all of their secrets.

"I think you're right," Devlin reassured her, coming forward to give her a brief hug and to shake her husband's hand. "You're going to be fine, both of you. If you have any setbacks, you know how to reach me, but something tells me that I won't be getting a call."

The two of them visibly relaxed, awkwardness gone.

"Well, thanks again," George added, passing a fat envelope to Devlin, then the two of them were exiting the office, giving him one final wave from the doorway as they left the reception area and stepped out into the night.

When they were gone, he opened the envelope and whistled at the cash bonus inside; definitely a pair of satisfied clients. Knowing that he had helped them and others like them was the only reason for his existence. Except for his admittedly unorthodox work, his life was, and had been, empty for the last thirteen years. He couldn't move on because he couldn't stop mourning. There was no gravestone to visit, no memorial to sit beside, no corpse to cry over. Death, with its finality, would be easier than what he lived with.

He slid the envelope into the hidden pocket of his black leather blazer before shrugging into the garment. When he had come here this afternoon, there was no rain and only a remote chance of it, so he would get wet but it didn't matter. His vehicle was only parked down the street and the elements didn't bother him; they made him feel, just for a moment, something.

The Scout Devlin drove was forty years old and, parked under a streetlight as it was, even the rain couldn't hide its many imperfections. One side of it was roughly beat up, with dents and patches of Bondo mingling with the faded original paint until it looked like a black eye three days after a punch. It was probably still better looking than he was. The right side of his face had been mangled and scarred in an accident years before. Thirteen years before. He had the money and the ability to have it repaired, but he wore the results like a badge. They were a part of who he was. Part of the punishment he deserved for what he had done.

He shook his head at the thought as he put the vehicle into gear and pulled away from the curb. The ironic thing about those scars was that he used them to remind himself of the dark and ugly side of his personality at the same time that they drew an almost avaricious interest from others. Women in particular seemed to love them.

By the time he reached his condominium on Pleasure Bay, the rain had stopped and the city was quiet. Few vehicles trolled the streets at this time of night. This part of Boston Harbor was wealthy, his condo was comfortable, and he took a perverse pleasure in living so close to the tough South Boston streets that spawned him.

His cell phone rang just after he entered his apartment.

"Talk to me," he said, throwing his keys on the kitchen table.

"No, you talk to me," the male voice on the other end of the call shot back automatically.

"Mac," Devlin breathed, relieved that it was his friend and foster brother, Ryan MacGilvary, and not another client. In his line of work he got calls at all hours of the night.

"Been out with a client?" Mac asked.

"Yeah." Devlin shrugged out of his jacket and hung it on the hook by the door. "What are you doing up this late?"

"Taking care of some paperwork at the office. Mostly staring out the window."

Mac could truly turn a pile of garbage into money and had done so several times over, which was why Devlin invested in his projects, but Mac's real job was running a first class fitness and training facility in a renovated mill on the river. It wasn't something that should have had him staying this late at night, but whenever Devlin asked about it, Mac got evasive. Someday he would find out what it was all about; in the meantime, there was probably a purpose for a call at this hour.

"So what's on your mind?" he questioned, grabbing a beer from the refrigerator and popping the top off before straddling a kitchen chair and taking a long draw of the dark brew as he sat down.

"I have a job for you," Mac said.

"Shoot."

"Someone that Lexie has become friends with."

"You've got to be kidding me," Devlin groaned. Mac was a person who collected strays, of the human variety, when they were broken and bleeding and needed to be cared for. He had done the same thing for Devlin thirteen years ago, so he appreciated that part of his best friend's nature, but this young woman was not likely to have friends that he wanted to work with.

When Mac was silent, Devlin gave in. "So *Lexie* knows someone who can use my services."

"I wish you wouldn't say her name like that," Mac sighed, referring to the lack of enthusiasm evident in Devlin's tone.

"I don't say it like that, not to her face." In truth, he couldn't say he had any one solid thing against the young woman, but he sometimes thought that she and her crowd were pretenders, just posing at being goth, candy goth, or whatever they liked to call themselves. Grabbing a notepad and pencil from the table, Devlin added, "So tell me."

"We don't know a lot. She's in her late twenties or early thirties. Shows up at the pharmacy every Sunday night at ten minutes to closing. Stands at the end of the line even if she was ahead of other customers."

"Avoidance. Gotcha."

"Covers her head and wears baggy clothes."

"Fear of sexuality."

"Never deviates from the routine."

"Trying to have control in some part of her life."

"Buys store brand products and only necessities. You know, toilet paper, paper towels, stuff like that."

"Denying herself pleasure."

"Parks in exactly the same spot every week."

"She'll get herself killed or attacked if she doesn't change things up."

"She was attacked. Kidnapped and held for weeks."

"Oh, Jesus," Devlin whispered, his insides going hollow. For a minute he couldn't breathe from the rush of memories threatening to overwhelm him. His vision went blurry, almost black, before he could work his way through it. Swallowing the constriction in his throat, he asked, "Are you sure she wants help?"

"Sure."

"Tell me why you're so certain, Mac."

"She noticed Lexie's forearms. Asked her if cutting helped relieve the pain."

Devlin dropped the phone on the table and grabbed the bridge of his nose, squeezing his eyes shut against the moisture that gathered behind his lids. He knew that feeling. Having so much pain on the inside that you couldn't express it and wondering why no one noticed that you were dying because you looked so normal on the outside.

"Dev? Dev!" Mac's voice came from the cell phone, concerned, urgent.

Devlin picked the handheld device up, put it to his ear, and took a deep breath. "I'm here," he finally answered.

"You okay, brother?"

Only Mac would ask that question because only Mac knew that what he was asking of his foster brother might actually be more than he could handle. Devlin had almost been lost to a darker side of himself thirteen years ago, and even though he had recovered enough to be a productive member of society, it had cost him in ways that most people didn't understand. Mac was the only one who did.

"Yeah, I'm okay," came the delayed response. Devlin put the pencil to the notepad and said, "Give me what you got."

It was no secret that Devlin disliked Lexie and that the feeling was mutual. From their first meeting the enmity had been there between them. He thought she was classless and crude; she thought the same thing about him. He had used his background in psychology to analyze the hostility between them and knew it stemmed from a rivalry for Mac's affections and a desire to protect him from the other one. Neither one of them thought the other was worthy of his esteem. Devlin knew that the feelings they shared were ridiculous. Mac was a great judge of character and when he gave to someone, he didn't give up on anyone else.

Understanding feelings was not the same as changing them,

though. The moment the big-boned young woman with the unnatural ebony hair stepped out of the pharmacy and crossed to the smoke break area the following day, he was filled with animosity. The curl of her black painted lips assured him that she was experiencing the same reaction, even before her belligerent greeting, "Dickhead."

"Bitch," he nodded, watching as she plopped down onto the bench across the aluminum table from him.

If Mac were present, he would already be calling for time out. Since he wasn't, and the niceties were over, the two of them got down to business, the sooner to be done with it. Devlin opened the new client folder and went through the paperwork with her; questionnaire, contract for services, insurance release forms if applicable, and clinician release forms that allowed him to talk with current and past care providers.

"Her doctor has to fill out a form?" Lexie asked with some surprise.

"If she's seeing one," Devlin confirmed. "It helps if I know her case history, diagnoses, meds, therapy that has been tried or that she's currently trying."

"Wow."

"What?" Devlin asked.

"This is just a lot more professional than I expected," she admitted.

It wasn't the first time that someone had reacted this way. Doctors and clients alike often thought he was just this side of legal.

"You thought I was a gigolo," he stated.

Lexie's kohl-rimmed blue eyes met his. "I have no idea what that means."

"A male prostitute. That I just fuck for a living," he elucidated, enjoying her discomfiture.

"Actually, I did."

He could have enlightened her. Told her that while he used surrogates on rare occasions, he wasn't one himself or told her that he didn't have sex with anyone, let alone clients. Instead he shrugged, closed the folder, and slid it across the table to her. "That's okay," he said, rising, "I thought you were too self-centered to ever notice someone else's pain."

"You also don't think I have a brain in my head," she accused.

"The jury is still out on that one. What I do think is that if you have one, you don't use it much."

"You're such an asshole."

Devlin held his tongue, because the two of them could go on like this all day long. Each had to have the last word. Again, the cerebral part of him knew better and he should have been able to control it, but it never worked out that way. He was also sorry that he had made that last comment because it reminded him of his own youth.

The barrage of memories unleashed by their short exchange was almost more than he could take as he drove the Scout across the city to Mac's place of business.

He had been sixteen years old and pulled into the police station for fighting. Again. "Do you want to be a fuck-up all your life, O'Malley?" Sergeant Webster had asked.

"Works for me," he had replied with a surly bite.

The big black man had leaned across the desk then, forcing Devlin to lean back in his chair or share breathing space. The cop knew what he was doing. After years of being shuttled around the inner and outer city from foster home to foster home, Devlin had a "thing" about people being in his face. In his space.

"You might have some people convinced that you're a dumb shit, but I know differently. There's a brain inside that head of yours and for some reason, you're too lazy to use it."

Devlin's only response was to stare belligerently at the cop.

"It's your choice, kid. Keep it up and I'll come to your funeral before you're even old enough to drink. But it doesn't have to be that way; it really is your choice."

"I'm not a kid," Devlin snapped, swiping the paperwork off the desk that held his court appointment date and toppling his chair on purpose as he rose. He left the police station without apology.

Sergeant Webster had made his point, though. When Devlin appeared before the judge a couple of weeks later, he agreed to do community service at a center for immigrants and aliens, one of those places that helped people who were new to the country find their way around without being completely taken advantage of. It was better than the alternative of spending time at the Deer Island pen, and he had something to prove to himself.

He had been at the center for less than a month when the cop paid him a visit. It was a toss-up as to who was more surprised, Devlin, because the man cared enough to check up on him, or Sergeant Webster, because the young man actually talked to him about his work at the center and didn't blow him off, but on that day an unlikely friendship began between the two of them. One that saw Devlin through the remaining years of high school and college and influenced him to go into law enforcement when he had earned his degree in psychology. He was just glad that Sergeant Webster died before seeing the mess he had made of that choice.

Chapter 2
Going Undercover

Devlin came back to the present when the road widened and the utilitarian streetlights changed to black lampposts in the old gas style. Dull gray buildings were replaced with marble, granite, and brick and he turned the Scout between the branches of a pair of ancient maple trees, looking dignified despite their nude spring status. A large parking lot opened up to the right and left, mostly full, but Devlin found a spot for his vehicle right next to a gleaming BMW convertible with vanity plates that spelled MAC. He smirked at the contrast between his best friend's car and his own multicolored piece of history.

Inside the renovated mill the receptionist greeted him with warm familiarity. "Hello, Mr. O'Malley, how are you today?"

"Fine, Mariah. Is he upstairs?" he asked.

"Yes. He's expecting you."

Devlin entered the antique elevator car beside her desk, hooked the accordion steel gate, then leaned back against the oak-paneled interior. He didn't have to hit the button for the fourth floor; Mariah had already done that for him using a console on her desk. The button for that floor didn't exist inside the car itself. If you had a key, you could get there, or you could be given clearance as he had just been.

The car came to a stop in the middle of a carpeted hall that extended in both directions. Devlin went to the last room on the right, passed through the unoccupied receptionist office, and found his friend in the inner room, gazing out the floor length windows behind his desk at the river and the city beyond.

Devlin knocked on the doorframe. Mac did not have his problem with surprises, but it still wouldn't feel right to just walk in unannounced.

"Dev!" the other man smiled, leaving his post to come around and thump him on the back in what passed as a hug between them.

"See anything good out there?" Devlin asked, knowing that when Mac stared into space, he was doing some of his best work. Planning his next project. Earning his next big profit, which the two of them shared as partners, though Devlin's contribution was a silent one.

"Possibilities, brother, possibilities," Mac responded, leaning back against his desk and crossing his feet at the ankles. "Did you go see Lexie?"

Devlin nodded. "Just came from there."

"Good. I have a feeling about this case. She could be the one."

"Don't start with me," Devlin warned. Mac wanted to see him settled, content and cared for but understood that he had to make peace with the past first. "You know it's never gonna happen."

"All right." Mac held up both hands in surrender. This was an old argument between them. Mac thought that a case would come along one day and provide the catharsis Devlin needed to forgive himself so that he could enjoy living again. His best friend probably thought that this was that case because the woman's experience was so similar to what Devlin couldn't forget.

A knock at the door made them both turn to find a freckled face below a mop of brown curls just visible above a large cardboard box that barely fit through the doorway. Devlin was closest to the young man, relieving him of his burden and putting it down on a side table. "Jesus, Gremlin, you work in a gym. You'd think you might build up some muscles eventually."

Pushing his glasses up, Mac's tech expert smiled at Devlin, unperturbed, and said, "It's never gonna happen."

"You were listening?" Mac scowled.

"Only heard the one line. I'm not here to eavesdrop on your conversations, boss."

"What *are* you here for?"

"To update your equipment. You said you'd be out to lunch, so

I figured this was probably the best time to do it."

"Good thinking. Ready, brother?" he asked Devlin, who nodded, and the two of them headed for the elevator.

"Later, Gremlin," Devlin said with a nod to the tech as he passed him.

"Uh-huh."

"Why do you call him that?" Mac asked when they were riding the car to the first floor.

"Gremlin? It's his game name. You didn't know he was a gamer?"

Mac shrugged.

"Did you know Lexie was a gamer?"

Now he had Mac's full attention, and he recognized the gleam in his best friend's eyes. "Forget it, brother. It's never gonna happen."

Mac just laughed at him.

Devlin remembered that laugh on Sunday night as he watched Lexie take care of customers in the pharmacy while waiting for his client to make an appearance. He could not imagine this big-boned, black haired woman with the scarred forearms and pierced flesh hitting it off with the wiry, freckled, bespectacled genius known as Gremlin, but the idea entertained him and helped pass the time while he pretended to be immersed in the books and magazine aisle.

It was eleven minutes to closing when Lexie drew his attention by rapping on the counter. He looked up to see the double doors of the pharmacy slide apart and a tall, spare figure dressed in a trench coat and wide-brimmed rain hat entered the store.

"Evening," Lexie greeted with a nod.

"Hello," came the muffled reply, then the client picked up a shopping basket and went into the paper goods aisle, unaware that Devlin followed her progress with the help of the store's big round security mirrors.

He watched as she selected generic paper towels and napkins from the top shelf. She was a tall woman and didn't need to reach to get them. When she bent to get store brand dish liquid, she used her knees instead of her waist, a graceful movement that allowed her to rise smoothly to her feet again. She seemed sure of her body, each action economical and clean, no clumsiness or hesitation at all. He recognized and admired the kinesthetic intelligence this showed.

She left that aisle for soaps and shampoos, selected a couple of things, then made her last stop in the first aid aisle before advancing to the register. A man approached at the same time from the other side of the store. He offered to let her go before him, but when she declined he shrugged and paid for his purchases.

Devlin checked the mirrors to make sure that there were no other patrons in the store. Assured that there were not, he emerged from the periodicals aisle and slipped quietly out of the building. He crossed the parking lot, past the smoke break area where he and Lexie had met earlier in the week, and stepped into the neighborhood bar and grill that backed up to the river. There he got a table and waited for the two women to conclude their business before joining him.

Lexie came in first, but the client was tall enough that he could see her face above the pharmacy clerk's head and she took his breath away. Finely arched light brown eyebrows, wide set blue eyes, high cheekbones, a pale oval of a face and that emaciated look so common to models and Eastern Europeans, all took him back to another girl, another time, thirteen years ago to be exact...

It was late autumn thirteen years before when, after finishing college the previous summer and spending the required weeks at police academy, Devlin found himself recruited as an undercover agent for the Commonwealth of Massachusetts. They were working in conjunction with federal agents to break an international crime ring working out of the New England coastal cities and he was perfect for the job. His past criminal activity, his work at the immigration center, his degree in psychology, and the fact that no one knew him as a cop yet, all added up to someone who could easily move through the underground community with little risk of detection as a spy.

He shaved his head and tattooed his upper arms with the Latin words ad servire and et tueri; to serve and protect in English. Mac told him he was an idiot, but he loved the irony of wearing words that could be viewed as gang related or a police pledge, depending on one's interpretation. Sergeant Webster just shook his head when Devlin showed them off to him.

"Be yourself, kid," he advised, wheezing the words from his couch where he lay dying of lung cancer. "Just act like the tough nut from South Boston who doesn't give a shit about anyone. They'll believe you because it's real."

"I'm not a kid," Devlin had responded, but without the bite he had once used when making that comeback. He knew Sergeant Webster was proud of him for the path he had chosen. A week later the older man died and when Devlin finally went undercover, his only outside contact was Mac.

The assignment was to infiltrate and reveal a white slave trade. Young women, most from the newly fractured Eastern European bloc, were coming to America for opportunities. What they found when they got here was very different, and most of them were simply processed through the coastal cities, then sold out of the country again.

Devlin had been introduced under the racist Irish nickname of Mick to Petr Kraus at a party in Attleboro. Kraus was a Czech immigrant who ran the Providence operations for the slave ring, and he was looking for an assistant. Business was booming. He couldn't be in two places at once, he complained to Devlin while they talked that night. Sometimes he was expected at the airport or had to meet with clients and he needed someone he could trust to watch over the girls while he did that.

They arranged to meet at a camp on Narragansett Bay where the girls were processed. It had the advantage of being not far from the cities where a lot of their clients stayed, having buildings and beds for large numbers, and being officially closed for almost ten months of the year. Kraus actually worked at the camp in the summer and in the off-season he was the caretaker, so it was easy for him to pretend that he was providing temporary shelter for immigrants just getting started in America. No one asked questions. The girls didn't speak English, so they were reliant on Kraus. By the time they figured out what was happening to them, it was too late; they had no way to communicate to authorities what was going on.

Devlin spent a week in late December at the camp, preparing the facility for the next batch of girls to arrive. He and Kraus bought food, chopped wood for the fireplace, and stocked up on other supplies; those needed for forging passports, medical records, and the like.

The girls came in the middle of the day. Because they had no idea what they were in for, they were smiling, happy, nervous, excited, anything but truly scared. Kraus put on a show, acting the magnanimous host, welcoming them with a big meal and lavish attention. Devlin sat at a long table, meeting with each one to take down her vital information, collect her passport, photograph her, and assign her to a room in the main lodge.

On the following day the girls were briefed on American life and culture. This charade involved watching an R-rated film and trying on swimsuits and other sexy clothing that, of course, they were photographed in. Then Kraus escorted them into the city for a sightseeing expedition. The next day followed a similar routine. Devlin worked during that time to create dossiers on each one; fake passport, new name, photographs, and medical records. By the third full day they returned from their expedition to find clients or client agents waiting to meet them.

The girls were introduced to these people, mostly men, as prospective employers, and went willingly with them for their "interviews". Some actually came out of the cabins assigned for this still not knowing what awaited them and blithely leaving in the company of their new boss. Others emerged with dazed looks in their eyes, bruises on their bodies, and shocked accusations spewing from their lips. Even then they thought there was some mistake. Kraus would surely protect them from this abuse; if not him, then Devlin. When they realized their mistake, and the betrayal sank in, they were already leaving.

"Good job, Mick," Kraus complimented Devlin when the last of the girls had departed with her escort. "Very good job!" He then paid Devlin, added a generous tip, and told him to be back in three days for the next "batch".

As soon as Devlin was off the grounds of the camp he steered his police issued coupe onto the shoulder of the road and threw up. All he wanted was to leave this place and never see it again. Quit right now. If he did that, they could try to get another plant into his position, but it would take months to do, and in that time hundreds of girls would come and go like those he had seen this week. Gone, and lost forever. So he got back into the car and drove to South Attleboro, where he unlocked the door to his police issued apartment and relayed all that he knew to his contacts who were already waiting there for him.

Several hours later he got on the T and headed north. He didn't even call Mac first. He didn't know if he could trust his emotions. Instead he got off at South Station and walked the few blocks to his friend's apartment. Using his spare key, he let himself in, only to find that Mac was enjoying the company of two very attractive young women. He took one look at Devlin's wrecked visage and sent them home in a taxi with a rain check.

Mac locked the door behind them before turning to look at his best friend pacing by the table. "Talk to me," he said quietly.

Devlin thought he could do it, but when he opened his mouth, nothing came out. He swallowed and tried again. Still nothing. He hung his head, squeezed his eyes shut against the moisture building there.

He hadn't been like this since they were kids in the same foster home and the "foster father" of the household raped him. He felt violated all over again. Though Mac couldn't know the details of what had happened this week, he knew exactly what to do. Crossing the room, he threw his arm around Devlin's neck, pulled the shaved head against his own shoulder, and held on to him. Devlin gripped his back, shaking with emotion.

It was some time before the storm passed. Devlin went limp against the other man, but he didn't let go. Mac nudged the side of his friend's head with his chin. "If you sit down, I'll start the shower. Okay?"

Devlin nodded silently. He didn't move, though, and Mac had to help him to the sofa before going to the bathroom and setting out a towel and cloth, starting the water and getting it to the right temperature. When he returned to the living area, Devlin was exactly as he had left him.

"It's ready," Mac said, waiting. Waiting to see if Devlin was going to be able to take care of himself, or if he even heard him.

Eventually Devlin rose from the sofa and moved into the bathroom. He could tell that Mac wanted to reach out and hold him again, but Devlin stepped around the other man, so emotionally fragile he was afraid that he would shatter at the slightest touch. So he left Mac to look on helplessly as he stepped into the steam-filled room and closed the door behind him.

Once inside the bathroom, Devlin stripped and stepped beneath the heated spray. He was dirty, inside and out, and he knew that the shower could run for days but he wouldn't be clean. That didn't stop him from scrubbing himself almost raw though. Even when the hot water ran out he would have kept going if Mac hadn't come into the room and turned the water off.

"Come on," his foster brother urged, holding out a bath sheet for Devlin to use.

Mac gave him a pair of sweat pants to put on when he was done toweling himself dry, then herded him into the bedroom where the covers were already turned down.

"Not exactly the hot night you had in mind," Devlin murmured as he sank onto the mattress.

"There will be others," Mac reassured him. He then turned off the lights, slid onto the other side of the bed, and held Devlin. "I love you, brother," he reassured him, and that's when the tears came. Not quiet, manly tears, but great wracking, noisy sobs. Devlin clung to his best friend and foster brother and slept only when there were no tears left to shed.

The next day he was drained, empty. Prone to occasional moodiness and sometimes quiet, this was still unusual for him, but Mac did not press him for details, instead doing his best to give him what he needed. They spent a few hours at the gym where Mac worked, went to a movie, walked the streets until snow began to fall and they could no longer feel their toes, then retreated to a corner bar to watch the Celtics play and listen to the crowd shout at the screen.

Mac had to work a full shift the following day. Devlin went in with him for a workout but spent the rest of the time in the apartment, watching television without seeing anything, wondering if he was strong enough for this job. In his mind he saw every one of those girls. He knew every name, their real names as well as their false names, and he saw every one of their faces as they left the camp; those that were shattered and betrayed, those that were eager and hopeful. He had no idea how he was supposed to eat or sleep, not knowing if they were eating or sleeping. He wondered how he would ever be able to live with his part in their destruction.

"You can't help any of them if you can't gather intel," his supervisor had told him during the debriefing. "We need enough to put these guys away. They can't walk for lack of evidence. This case has to be so tight, so thoroughly investigated, that there will be no chance of them getting out on bail and taking the first plane out of the country. That's where you come in, Mick. If you screw it up, they're all lost. Forever."

Late in the afternoon he went to the bank and deposited his pay and tip into the account that he had opened for just this purpose. Then he returned to the apartment, left Mac a note saying he was going back to South Attleboro, and hopped on the T.

Kraus must have suspected his feelings about their work the previous week. When Devlin arrived at the camp for another round, Kraus slapped him on the back and said, "Don't worry, Mick. It gets easier. And they only cry at first. Then, if they're smart, they get used to it and do as they're told. They have a better life with their owners than they had in the old country. At least they have food, clothes, a warm bed. They get paid for their work. It's better this way."

The second week was easier for Devlin. Not because of Kraus' words; he didn't believe for a moment that the girls were better off in their new situations. He just found a way to dull his emotions enough to get through what he had to get through. But he didn't pretend. Let Kraus be the jolly host while he was the quiet, businesslike one. He couldn't smile at these girls, make eye contact and small talk with them, then send them off to be raped and sold into hell.

At the end of the week when they were all gone, Kraus told him that it had been another good week, gave him another big tip, but told him to loosen up over the weekend. Get a girl. Get laid. He didn't tell the Czech that since he started this job, surrounded by half-clad nubile females, he could not even get an erection. He had tried.

Instead of going directly to South Attleboro from Mac's apartment, he had made a stop along the way and dropped in on an old acquaintance. The woman was between boyfriends and happy to see him and at first he thought he had had found the perfect therapy; an afternoon of sexual escapism. They talked a little, petted some, moved into her bedroom, and from there everything fell apart.

Devlin couldn't get aroused. If his eyes were open, he saw the girls at the camp. He still saw them with his eyes closed. So he tried harder, redoubling his efforts at lovemaking and concentrating on the woman he was with. Even then his mind wandered. He pictured the two of them spread out on her bed. A receptive woman who knew what she was doing but didn't know the man she was with.

She didn't know that he was there seeking absolution. Didn't know he had taken part in the destruction of innocence. When she found him limp and unresponsive, she sympathized with his condition. Told him it was okay, not to worry, maybe he was coming down with something. He let the idea serve as the explanation because he couldn't tell her the truth. Just like he couldn't tell Kraus that getting laid wasn't an option for him. The man would not have understood or been happy with him.

Chapter 3

Arrival

Devlin's superiors were certainly not happy with his disposition during the debriefing. They again lectured him on the importance of what he was doing and added the caution that he couldn't make Kraus suspicious. Yes, even criminals have a conscience, they noted, but not one that would get in the way of doing the job and they worried that he was in danger of blowing it by letting his get the best of him.

He didn't go to see Mac. Instead he stayed in his apartment in South Attleboro. He picked at his guitar but no music came, watched television but saw nothing, and slept. When Mac called, he answered with the usual, "Talk to me," because Mac was the only one who would call.

"No, you talk to me," Mac responded.

"I just needed to be alone for a couple of days," he explained.

"You're okay, though?"

"Yeah. I'll be okay."

"You can always come home, Dev. No matter what they tell you. If it's too hard on you, you can always walk away."

Devlin doubted that. Already he could feel himself falling toward some deep, dark place, a place that could swallow him alive, where he would be lost forever, and he didn't know if he would go over the edge or pull back in time to save himself.

"Dev?"

"I hear you, brother," he reassured Mac. "If I need you, I'll call."

But Devlin didn't call. He went two more rounds, getting duller, getting harder, proving to Kraus that he was efficient and could be trusted at his job. On his days off he went to South Attleboro, gave his report, and holed up in his apartment with nothing but the television and his guitar for company.

Something changed after that, and he wasn't sure what, but he found himself getting angry with the girls that came through the camp. Were they really that naïve? Were their families really that stupid?

They had a chance that he had never had. When the social worker delivered him to the foster house from hell, he had been a child. He couldn't choose where he went or who he stayed with, but these girls could. From everything he had heard and seen, they had chosen to come to America.

He had seen innocent immigrants at the center he worked at, but these girls beat anything he had encountered there. They were lambs about to be slaughtered and none of them saw it coming. Would they really have trusted two strange men in their own countries, he wondered.

Devlin had studied enough Freud that he eventually recognized his feelings for what they were; displacement. A defense mechanism marked by the transference of emotion from one target to another. He knew that the anger really came from his own frustration at having to watch what was happening at the camp and not being able to do anything about it.

He was a police officer. His job was about keeping people safe. Keeping them free from the kind of harm that he was now involved with. He was supposed to serve and protect. Help others the way that Mac and Sergeant Webster had helped him. Instead he was working with the criminals, violating the most basic of human rights, and the only outlet for his roiling emotions were the victims themselves.

The anger soon changed to disdain. It had to. Like the profound grief that had driven him to Mac's apartment that first weekend, it would consume him if he let it. So he adopted this new emotion instead, one that took a lot less energy, one that wouldn't threaten his sanity. Much like when he was a kid, he took on the persona most likely to help him operate, protect himself, survive. Only, where the young Devlin had become surly and aggressive, the adult Devlin became contemptuous and apathetic.

He still worked in his business-like manner, but he no longer remembered their faces or their names as they passed through his processing line. He no longer cared that they were being sent into a life of hell. It served them right. Anyone that stupid deserved what she got.

Again Kraus seemed to know what was happening with him, seemed to sense the demons riding his shoulders. When they had prepared the camp for the sixth batch of girls to arrive, he told Devlin that he should make the trip to the airport and meet their contact there.

"Why the change?" Devlin asked, suspicious.

"You need to get out. See more of the operation. If we keep growing, we'll need two sites, and you could run the other one. So you meet Stanislaw, get the girls, pick one for yourself while you're at it."

"Pick one?"

"Sure. Is not good for a man to look at fresh young girls all day and not have one of his own. So you pick one. Keep her."

"Keep her? For the week?" Devlin queried.

"For the week, for a month," he shrugged. "Whatever you want. She is yours. You do what you want with her."

It was a long drive to Philadelphia in the camp van. They rotated international airports so the authorities wouldn't get suspicious, and this week it was Philadelphia. That gave Devlin five hours to consider the suggestion. Was the Czech right? Would having a woman of his own make it easier for him to get through the job he had? That didn't mean he wanted one of the girls that came through the camp, but she would probably be better off with him than with some of the lechers they were sold to. Especially the female buyers; the female buyers were the worst because the girls mistakenly thought they would have some sympathy for their situation. When they instead inspected and touched the girls as if they were livestock, revulsion and horror replaced that last bit of hope. It was the ultimate betrayal to them; betrayal by one of their own. Was Devlin a better alternative to that?

By the time he arrived at the airport, he found himself considering Kraus's suggestion. He knew that Kraus slept with at least one girl each week if not more, but Devlin would rather have just one and, again, the other man had read him correctly in this.

Maybe he could pick one of the more experienced ones. That way he would not be raping innocence because, in spite of the hardening of his emotions, he could still distinguish between being party to someone else's demise and being directly responsible for it. She would be spared from a much worse fate. He would not be alone all the time. It would really be better than the alternative for both of them.

Devlin had probably never done so much rationalizing in his life, he realized as he pulled the van into a parking spot.

He found their contact easily enough, a big Russian all in black, surrounded by a dozen young women wearing bright green t-shirts that said Camp Sunshine on them. They were chattering away excitedly, remarking on everything they saw, admiring outfits that passersby were wearing, and generally enjoying their first taste of America. Devlin introduced himself to the Russian and they went through a security check with one another before herding their charges out to the van.

At the beginning of the ride the girls were eager to take in everything they saw, but it was a five-hour trip that began with a one-hour traffic gridlock, so by the time they were halfway to Rhode Island, it was dark and most of them were asleep. Devlin was glad for the quiet. He needed it to get his head in order.

Not one of the girls fit the description he had settled on. None bore the look of experience he had hoped to find and he was wrestling with both an acute sense of relief and a deep disappointment. To have gone through all the mental machinations it took to convince himself that he was doing the right thing, or at least an acceptable thing, only to have the opportunity lost was hitting him harder than he expected.

The only break in the monotonous drive was the couple of times he had to pull over on the side of the road for one of the girls to be carsick. Eventually she moved up to the front seat, right where he could see her.

That's when he made his decision.

She was nothing like the woman he had decided on. Her name was Masha Wozny, and she came from Kharkhiv, Ukraine. At sixteen she was one of the youngest to go through the camp in the weeks Devlin had worked there. She was tall, lean, had long light brown hair, heavy dark eyebrows over hazel eyes, and a wide mouth with a big, eager looking smile when she thought it was expected. Otherwise, she was rather solemn looking. She did not seem to completely trust him or the Russian, and he marveled that such a young girl should be able to see what the older girls were oblivious to. It didn't matter, though; her fate was already sealed.

"You like one?" Kraus asked after they were settled for the night at the lodge.

"I do."

"Which one?"

"The skinny Ukrainian girl with the long hair. Big eyes."

"Ahhh," Kraus smiled. "A good choice for you, I think. Very young. Trainable."

"We'll see," Devlin remarked, but for the first time since working with the Czech, his smile was a real one.

Chapter 4

The Client

Looking at the woman in the restaurant now, Devlin could not believe that he had ever thought that way. That he had ever let the darkness take hold of him to such an extent that he became the monster from his childhood; someone with total disregard for the feelings of another human being, a helpless person dependent on him for her welfare. But he would help this woman and any other woman in a situation like hers. He helped as many as he could. For Masha; for the one he couldn't help.

"Hello, Melissa," he greeted the client, reaching across the table to shake her hand as she took a seat on the other side.

"Mr. O'Malley," she said softly, casting her eyes down at her lap, keeping her hands at her side.

Even less open than expected; he could deal with that.

"Lexie suggested that we meet here, but if you would be more comfortable somewhere else?"

"This is fine," she said, but didn't lift her eyes.

"Okay. Lexie?" He looked up at the pharmacy clerk, still hovering near the table. "The rest of our meeting is confidential."

"Oh! Sure." She backed up and disappeared into the crowd.

Devlin turned back to his client. "We won't have very long to talk tonight, so let's get some of the formalities out of the way. The first thing I need is your paperwork."

She reached into her coat pocket and pulled out the forms, rolled up in a rubber band, and handed them across the table to him. She was careful to avoid any contact between her hand and his when he took them from her.

He scanned them for completion and vital information. Then he turned to the notes provided by her psychologist, surmising almost right away that her practitioner did not understand the real world as much as she understood clinical terms and diagnoses. Finally he read Melissa's narrative, written in her own hand. It was succinct. Raped. Held captive for three months. Unable to be intimate since then, in any way, with anyone.

"It looks like we have a lot to talk about," he said, rolling the forms up again. "Let me walk you to your car and we can make a follow-up appointment."

She seized up immediately.

"We can find Lexie and have her accompany us if that makes you feel better."

She looked at the crowd, uncertain.

"We can meet in public places as much as you want, but Lexie cannot accompany you for your therapy sessions. At some point you will have to give me your trust. It's the only way that I can help you."

She looked back to him, her bright blue gaze wavering slightly but trying valiantly to maintain contact with his own.

"Come," he suggested, rising from the chair and motioning her to precede him out of the room.

One more small hesitation, then she complied.

They met three days later at a diner in the middle of the afternoon. Not a busy time. Not a busy place. Melissa had admitted to avoiding crowds of people, but Devlin knew that crowds were not intimate. He had chosen this time and place deliberately so there was less opportunity for her to spend her time looking at everyone else and not having to give any of her attention to him. He had also purposely arrived after her so that she would be forced to acknowledge him on his arrival.

"Good afternoon, Melissa," he greeted as he slid into the seat opposite her own.

"Mr. O'Malley," she returned, her throat sounding dry. She

took a sip of water from her glass while he shucked his leather coat and rested his hands on the table. He had square hands with blunt tipped fingers and wore leather gauntlets on both wrists. She fixed her attention on them.

"Have you ordered anything?" he asked.

"No. I wasn't sure if we were eating."

"We are," he assured her, turning his head and catching the eye of the waitress behind the counter.

Devlin knew what he was doing. This woman was afraid of any kind of intimacy. Having to sit across from him, look at him whenever she looked up, and share a meal with him, was intimate. Some people might have thought that a quiet interview in an office with music playing would be the best atmosphere, but they would be wrong. They also would not be able to help her with her problem.

Over his Reuben sandwich and her clam chowder, he prompted, "Tell me about him."

"Who?" she jerked, startled, eyes going wide in the oval of her face.

"The man who held you against your will."

She grew still and placed her soup spoon carefully on the napkin beside her bowl, adjusting it until it was exactly aligned with the design of the paper fabric, then smoothing the folded corners of her placemat, one at a time, until they were just so. Her throat moved once, a single nervous swallow, then hesitantly her blue eyes lifted to meet his own.

"What do you want to know?"

"Everything," he replied. "Was he old? Fat? Cruel? Dirty? Did he drug you?"

She played with the corners of the placemat again. He waited patiently for several moments, and just when he thought no response was forthcoming, he heard the faintest whisper pass her lips. "No."

Devlin put down the remains of his sandwich. He reached across the table and placed his large hands over the slender, blue-veined fingers that continued to flirt with the table decoration, forcing them to be still. She didn't like the contact at all, but it got her attention. "I need to see you when you answer, Melissa. I asked you several questions. Do you mean no to some of them, or no to all of them?"

"No to all of them," she admitted, in a voice that was even quieter than before.

"You're still not looking at me," he said patiently. "Look at me."

Slowly blue eyes met his own, shame evident in them, her face filled with consternation.

"Why does it bother you to tell me that?" he asked. "Just because he wasn't any of those things doesn't mean he wasn't a kidnapper. A rapist. He held you against your will and used you without permission. That isn't your fault. None of it was your fault."

"I know," she agreed readily. Too readily. "That's what my other therapists told me."

"But you don't believe them. Is that why you came to me?"

"No, I believe them," she rushed to say, again too quickly. Saying what she thought he wanted to hear. What she had been convinced was the right thing to say under the circumstances, but her flickering gaze revealed the lie for what it was.

"I don't believe you," he stated, releasing her hands and sitting back in the booth.

"What?" she asked, dismayed by his pronouncement and his withdrawal.

"You're not being honest with me. I don't know what you're hiding, but you're hiding something and until you can share what it is, I can't help you."

He stood and tossed some bills onto the table beside his plate.

"That's it?" she questioned, shocked by his actions.

"Yes," he agreed. "Until you are ready to level with me, I can't help you."

Placing his hands on either side of the table he leaned down so that he could make eye contact with her and not risk anyone overhearing their conversation. With so few people in the restaurant at this hour, even quiet sound could carry a long way.

Immediately she retreated as far back into the booth as she could go, almost as if they were nose to nose instead of separated by a few feet of polished wood. Devlin slowly removed his hands from that surface and held them out at his sides. The way a person does when they want to prove they are unarmed. Just as slowly he stood, not wanting to trigger a flight response in her. "I'd like to help you, Melissa," he said gently. "Really, I would. But I like to cut right to the chase with my clients, so I'm not going to treat you any differently. Your other therapists haven't worked, or you wouldn't have ended up here, with me. So you are looking for help, but you still think that you can control the situation. That's not how it works." He paused and waited while she absorbed this. After a moment he continued, "If I am your therapist, you are putting yourself in my care and trusting that I know what is best for you. That's a lot to ask, I know, but it's the only way that this can work."

Melissa said nothing though she relaxed into her seat, no longer looking at him like he was a threat. Devlin took a business card from his inside jacket pocket and placed it on the table next to her. It was simply inscribed, with only his last name and a phone number.

"Call me when you are ready to get to work."

Devlin knew that he had pushed her hard even though it was for her own good. It might have been too far; if it was she would go back to seeing people in clinical offices who sat far enough away from her that her personal space would never be violated. She would tell them what they wanted to hear and they would tell her things that ensured she remained in fearful isolation. On the other hand, he might have pushed her just far enough; enough to make her pick up the phone and follow through on whatever had led her to ask Lexie about cutting and the potential relief it brought.

After leaving the diner, Devlin drove across town to Mac's place and the two of them shared a sparring match in the "dungeon", the underground boxing facility that was part of Mac's establishment. It was Devlin's favorite part of the operation. When he needed to get his adrenaline up to where it matched the churning of his emotions, boxing provided the perfect release for him.

"I take it she got to you," Mac commented when they were finished, dripping with perspiration, and headed into the shower room.

"Yeah, I guess so," Devlin admitted. He hadn't known how much until he arrived here.

"Can you help her?"

"If she'll let me."

"Something tells me this will work out, Dev."

"What makes you say that?"

"She reached out once already; she must be in need of your particular brand of help or she wouldn't have come looking for it."

"Maybe." Dev was skeptical.

"Come on, brother, you know I'm always right. Trust me."

Chapter 5
Descent Into Darkness

Devlin should have remembered that and trusted Mac thirteen years ago, he admitted to himself as he drove across the city to his condo on the bay. When Mac told him that he should walk away from the case if it was too much for him, he should have run. Instead, he had listened to Kraus and his advice to take a girl for his own.

He had fun "courting" Masha, but she didn't make it easy. With their sightseeing and cultural exposure, he only saw her at night, so he paid a lot of attention to her then and made his interest obvious. The other girls, thinking he was "cute", giggled and teased her, but Masha was uncomfortable with it. She clung to the security of the group and avoided him whenever possible. When it wasn't possible, she was polite but not encouraging.

Devlin actually took perverse pleasure in saying outrageous things to her that she had no hope of understanding. By the third day he found the erotic talk and anticipation of what was to come were both giving him a hard-on, and he marveled at how this skinny young thing could do for him what the more willing and voluptuous girls had not been able to since he began this assignment.

On the night of the interviews, he took a reluctant Masha into a cabin and explained that she was too young for any of the jobs that were open. It took some time, with the language barrier, but eventually she comprehended what he was saying and, again after some time, let him know that she couldn't disappoint her family. They were counting on her.

He shushed her, sat on the bed next to her, and pulled her against his side.

Immediately she stiffened.

Devlin made sure that his touch was light and that he didn't move his hands in any way. It took only moments for her to relax and accept his embrace as simply one of comfort.

He was beginning to enjoy himself. *A lamb to the slaughter*, he thought, and kissed her temple.

She jerked her head back.

Devlin smiled reassuringly, used his index finger to lift her chin and looked into her wide hazel eyes. "It's okay, Masha, baby," he almost purred. "You and I are going to be good friends before this night is over. Real good friends." Still with his hand at her chin, he leaned forward and gave her a brief kiss on the lips.

This time she jerked back and as far away from him as she could given the wall at her back and his body blocking her exit from the bed.

He followed her, advancing slowly across the mattress until his hands were placed on either side of her hips and his body loomed over hers. She kicked out at him. Devlin simply lay down, trapping her lower limbs with his weight. She pushed at his shoulders and shrieked at him. He moved closer, nuzzling the curve of her cheek, the side of her neck. She tried to grasp a fistful of his hair to pull his head away. There wasn't enough to hold onto and her hands slid over the stubbly surface. Instead she bucked against him with her torso.

It turned him on. His cock leaped in reaction and he jerked back to stare down at her, amazed.

She looked at him warily, probably wondering what he was going to do next. He might have lifted his torso off her own and taken his mouth away, but she was a smart girl and there was no hiding the lust in his eyes. His blood literally sang with excitement. At last he could feel something and she was responsible. She would never get away now.

"Mick!" a shout at the door interrupted them, and before he had time to stand up Kraus was entering the cabin.

"The stupid pipe burst at the lodge," Kraus complained. "You know anything about plumbing?"

Devlin knew a little. After a brief discussion it was clear that even his limited amount of knowledge was a lot more than the other man had, so he agreed to go and check it out. He explained to Masha that she should stay, threw on his coat, and headed for the main building.

He had been working for a while, stuffed into the crawlspace beneath the kitchen of the lodge, when he realized that Kraus was no longer with him. Muttering a few choice words about laziness, he put the flashlight between his teeth and followed the line of plumbing with his eyes, looking for breaks.

Being alone gave him time to think about the scene that Kraus had interrupted. Despite his decision to "save" Masha and make her his companion, Devlin regretted that kiss. She was a sixteen year-old girl in a strange country without anyone to protect her. She needed his protection and instead he had acted like the pervert who used to take him into his workshop when he was too young to resist and Mac was not around to stop him. He had relished her fear and confusion. It had excited him, made her the most exciting challenge he had ever known, one he was determined to master in that moment.

Devlin knew from experience it was that very fear and resistance that turned his foster father on. The comparison made his blood run cold. There were so many victims of abuse who became abusers themselves, but he had never thought he would be one of them. Thought his moral compass was too sure. That he could never be pulled down into that dark place where evil ruled and conscience disappeared.

Calling himself a sick bastard and vowing to never touch her again, Devlin hurried to finish the repair job. He had to get back to the cabin and try to explain things to her.

He was several yards away when he heard her.

"Ne! Ne!" she cried, and for the second time that night his blood ran cold.

Devlin burst into a run.

The scene inside the cabin was everything he feared it would be. Kraus was on the bed, straddling a naked Masha, his hands fisted in her hair to hold her in place while his cock slammed into her, in and out, and she screamed, "Ne!" at the top of her lungs, tears running down the side of her face and into her long brown hair.

"You son of a bitch," Devlin snarled, hurling himself at the bed and the other man.

He ripped him from her body. Devlin threw Kraus to the floor and immediately hauled the half naked man up again, shaking him just like a dog shakes a stuffed animal, then burying his fist in the rapist's belly.

Devlin was finally free of pain. Everything that had happened in the last few weeks disappeared as he pounded the other man, enjoying it. There was no thought given to the fact that he was beating up his boss. That he might be jeopardizing the undercover operation. There was certainly no guilt. Masha was his, given to him to be exclusively his, not shared, not taken back and, despite his earlier behavior, his to protect from harm.

When the other man finally stopped fighting back, Devlin tossed him away, watching without sympathy as Kraus slid down onto the floor. Both of them were breathing hard.

"So, you like this one," Kraus managed to choke out when he finally staggered to his feet. "Okay, okay," he added, waving a hand and nodding his head. "She's yours."

"Don't touch her again," Devlin growled.

"No problem," Kraus agreed, opening the door. "She's yours." Then with a satisfied grin on his battered face, he added, "I just broke her in for you."

Devlin was sitting in the Scout in front of his condo, staring blindly at the joggers and dog walkers enjoying Castle Island and the bay despite the overcast day, lost in his memories. Until that night he had not known the darkness that lived inside him. Had not known how close it was to the surface, how weak he was against it, or how easily it could take hold of him.

A jet flew overhead on its way out of Logan Airport, reminding him of where he was and in what time. He stepped out of the vehicle, locked the doors, and crossed the road to his condo. It was a second floor corner unit, so he had to enter a key into the first door, a code at the door to the stairs, then a key at the top of the stairs to his condominium apartment. As nice as it was, it was still in South Boston and the only reason the petty criminals left him alone was because the Scout was unique, recognizable, and pretty much worthless. Even the tires had no resale value, since they were an old narrow size that didn't fit the new sport utility vehicles.

Once inside the condo, Devlin threw his keys on the small table before the window, added his cell phone, and was about to grab a beer from the refrigerator in the galley kitchen when his gaze fell to the guitar hanging on the wall. It had been months since he had even tried to play. Yet he took the case down now, flipped it open, and removed the instrument. A black pick with gold logo lettering rested in the frets and he slid it out, tuned the guitar for a few minutes, then found himself singing Wicked Games by Chris Isaak. It was an old song. He hadn't thought of it in years, but the lyrics were perfect for his melancholy mood.

> "The world was on fire and no one could save me but you.
> It's strange what desire will make foolish people do.
> I never dreamed that I'd meet somebody like you.
> And I never dreamed that I'd lose somebody like you."

He moved on to the refrain and wondered, as he often did, if he would have even noticed Masha in another setting. If she had shown up at the immigrant center where he volunteered, would he have thought her woman enough for him and actually courted her, or dismissed her as a skinny girl with big eyes.

> "What a wicked game to play, to make me feel this way.
> What a wicked thing to do, to let me dream of you."

Devlin's fingers stilled on the guitar strings. A smile that was no smile at all briefly crossed his damaged face. Few people would find the same irony in the lyrics that he did. Wicked. To people in Boston wicked meant good, fine, exceptional. He wished he could feel any of these things.

The buzzing of his phone was a welcome distraction from the dark mood he so often slipped into.

"Hello?" he greeted, not recognizing the number.

"Mr. O'Malley?" a female voice questioned from the other end of the call.

"Speaking," he growled, wishing it was another female, lost to his past, one with a Ukrainian accent.

"This is Melissa."

"Hello, Melissa." He had recognized her voice, of course, but was still surprised that her call had come so soon after their parting; still disappointed that it wasn't another voice. "What can I do for you?"

"I'd like to see you again."

"Okay." The professional Devlin took over. He arranged for their next meeting to be in his office so that they could discuss a treatment plan. He gave her directions, and when they ended the call, he turned off his cell phone and stared out the window at the people on Castle Island without seeing them at all.

The next day his schedule was full. He saw three clients in the morning, all couples. The first, in their mid-thirties, had fertility issues and had a standing appointment with him for every Thursday because the weekend began on Friday and weekends brought a lot of stress to their relationship. After them he saw an older couple trying to enjoy marital life following colostomy surgery, and last he saw a young couple trying to get past religious taboos that had them so convinced sex was bad that even within marriage they could not enjoy it.

In the afternoon he testified as an expert witness for a plaintiff who had lost his legs and his ability to enjoy conjugal relations with his wife as the result of a preventable industrial accident. From there he joined a social worker to evaluate two children who had been molested by their stepfather, and finally he took a break for dinner.

The meal was quick, because he had agreed to meet professors in Salem at the state university there to serve as one member of a professional panel on post-traumatic stress and relationships. It took an hour to get there, the discussion was an hour long, followed by half an hour of chatting, then he was finally heading home.

The light drizzle from earlier in the day had turned into sheets of freezing rain. The low salt areas were treacherous, with heavy moisture rolling in off the Atlantic, and he needed all of his faculties to make the drive. So he shouldn't have been able to slip into the past, but the combination of cold spring weather along with the monotony of staring at the windshield wipers rhythmically crossing before his eyes made it easy for him to move into that semi-hypnotic state where memories always waited for him.

Chapter 6
Wounds That Scar

Masha had run, of course; any sane girl would have after being used like that. Devlin had tried at first to comfort her, but she became hysterical and scrambled as far from him as she could, so in the end he stepped away, brought her a glass of water, gave her a nightshirt to wear, sat in a chair beside the bed and watched helplessly as she cried herself to sleep.

When she cried, he thought... at least she can cry. Unlike himself. He hadn't cried since that night at Mac's apartment. He couldn't. So he let her cry for both of them.

Early the next morning she got up to use the bathroom and somehow managed to crawl out the tiny window to flee into the forest. Unfortunately for her, he had a clear view of her escape from the front door of the cabin where he was looking out on a light layer of freshly fallen snow. Also unfortunate for her, she had no idea where they were located. With new snow on the ground and no shoes on her feet Devlin could easily track her, and with no sun in the sky and very little change in elevation as far as the eye could see she was directionless. She crossed the same stream twice, circling back around a stand of leafless hardwood trees, and would have plunged into a fairly deep pocket of ice water if he hadn't grabbed her by her long hair and pulled her to a stop. When he got his other arm around her, he let go, but his hand came away with several strands of light brown hair stuck to it and that gave her one more thing to hate him for as he dragged her back to the cabin.

Afraid that if he left her she would just try to run again, he found a toolbox in the closet and nailed the bathroom window shut. Then he locked her inside the room and, to protect her from anyone else, locked the outside door of the cabin as well. He had to get to the lodge to help Kraus with the other girls and their departure.

Kraus was waiting for him, sporting a bruised face but an ear-splitting grin. "You okay, Mick?" he asked as if nothing had happened.

Devlin grunted something in reply, taking his seat at the table where he worked.

"Don't get upset. I did you a favor," the other man said, slapping him on the back and tempting Devlin to hit him again. "Really," Kraus assured him. "You see, she hate me now. If she hate me, she won't hate you."

It was a couple of hours before they finished. When Devlin returned to the cabin he found Masha curled up in the corner of the bathroom between the vanity and the commode, eyes closed in sleep. As soon as the now open door landed against the wall, those large hazel eyes came open with a snap and her body jerked upright.

"It's okay, Masha, baby," he soothed, for the first time not really sure what to do with her.

The excitement of the previous night was gone. The anger of the previous night was gone. For the first time, he was uncertain what he was feeling. He was uncertain of exactly what to do, but he could not leave her in the corner of the bathroom for the rest of the day, so he motioned for her to stand and join him in the main room. In response she curled in on herself, narrowed eyes shooting daggers of accusation at him.

Devlin sighed. Of course this would have to be done the hard way.

Crouching down in front of her, he reached for her arm with one hand, for her leg with the other, and she came out kicking and screaming. Literally. Her bare feet were flailing, her nails scratching, she even tried to use her teeth on any part of his body she could reach. After suffering several minor wounds he gave up on any attempts to reassure her and simply hauled her to her feet, not giving her time to recover before throwing her over his shoulder and moving out into the other room.

She tried to stiffen against him, but from that position there was little she could do and she just ended up trembling instead.

Devlin was under no illusions about her strength or her spirit, though. He knew that as soon as he put her on her feet she would either attack or run. Fight or flight. Natural reactions to the situation, but neither one would change it and she might actually do harm, to him or to herself.

Spying a length of unused rope on the table where he had left it that morning, Devlin snatched it up with one hand while holding her pinned against his shoulder with the other. He knew he had to work quickly so he cut a short length of the rope and created a running noose knot on each end. Then, without warning he plopped her down on the table and, while she was catching her balance, slipped the knots around her wrists.

She screeched. Masha jumped up off the table and yanked at her hands, which only made the knots pull tighter. Frantically looking around, she spied the knife he had used and darted for it. Devlin swore and snatched it away just in time. He was not sure if she meant to use it on him or to cut the rope, but he could not take any chances. The girl was obviously resourceful and not to be underestimated.

Cognizant of this, he grabbed her around the waist from behind with one arm and grabbed the remaining rope from the table with the other. He ran that under the length connecting her wrists, then stood on a chair and tied both ends of it to a hook in the ceiling. She pummeled him with her fists while he did it. Tried to kick the chair out from under him. Bit him in the thigh.

"You little bitch," he hissed as the pain of the bite set in, and because of that he pulled the rope taut, forcing her up on to her tiptoes. Her hazel eyes went wide. *Good*, he thought, letting her stay in that position for a moment before tying the rope so that she had several feet of slack. He stepped down off the chair and moved the piece of furniture well out of her reach.

Masha crumpled to the floor. A girl could only take so much, he supposed, but he had no plans to underestimate her again. Devlin left her there while he went into the bathroom and started filling the tub. A bath would probably go a long way to making her feel clean. Having been raped himself, he knew how important that was.

He had washed for days. No matter how many showers he took, he could not wash away the memory of hands on his body, hands he tried to push away. He could not forget the agony of that first invasion, the violation of a place he could not even reach to clean, but he tried anyway. He knew from psychology classes that it was part of rape trauma syndrome. He knew from experience that it didn't work, that the feeling of washing away the filth left imprinted on his body only lasted a moment, but he kept trying anyway. Just as she would want to try.

At least he had Mac. His best friend and the closest thing he had to a brother had not only taken the pedophile's attention away from him, he had eventually beat the guy to a pulp once Devlin was safely out of the home. For that Mac had spent a few months at Deer Island House of Correction and discovered his love of working out while Devlin had continued to rebel until he ended up sitting across the desk from Sergeant Webster.

The old man would be ashamed of him now, he thought as he returned to the main room and scooped Masha up off the floor. Her eyes were glazed, her body unresponsive. She weighed next to nothing. He used the knife to sever the ceiling rope and carried her into the bathroom. Putting her down on the toilet seat, he sliced through the rope around her wrists and took off her nightshirt. She offered no resistance. A bad sign, he thought.

Lifting her again, he slid her into the full tub of warm water and, when she did nothing but sit there, he grabbed the soap and cloth from the shelf. Devlin dipped the cloth into the water, built up a good lather with the yellow bar and reached out to wash her.

He expected resistance. In fact, he expected her to come flying out of the tub at any moment. Either she would try to drown him or she would hurt herself trying to get out of the room. But she did not even move.

That was when he discovered that he could actually still feel something.

He had washed her hair, scrubbed her back and skimmed her front, then helped her to her feet to wash her legs. As soon as the cloth reached the juncture of her thighs, she cried out. Not a cry of objection, which he would have expected, but a cry of pain. Her body jerked away from his touch. Her face tightened and she bit her lower lip.

Moving cautiously now, Devlin tapped the insides of her thighs until she separated them enough for him to look at her there. What he saw disgusted him and showed rape for the act of violence that it was. Masha was bruised, swollen, and bloodied. It was a wonder she could walk at all. Devlin swallowed hard, just looking. Part of him wanted to turn away and vomit at both the damage that had been done to her and the fact that he was just as guilty as the perpetrator. But that wouldn't help her. So instead he worked as gently as he could, dabbing at her flesh to clean her. As soon as that was done he pulled the plug and let the water drain from the tub. He wrapped her in a big towel and again carried her, this time to a chair by the wood stove.

She sucked in her breath when he placed her on the seat despite the care he took in doing so.

Now what, he thought. What could he possibly do for this girl? How could he make her comfortable? Make her feel safe? Make up for what he had almost done and what Kraus had done?

He went with the most prosaic of remedies — food. She hadn't eaten all day, so he could begin with that.

Masha was able to take only a few spoonfuls of soup from the bowl he held before turning her head away. Then he put one of his own flannel shirts on her and a pair of his wool socks because her own were thin, providing no heat. He dried her hair with the towel, changed the sheets on the bed, settled her beneath the covers and, after locking her in again, went up to the lodge to see if there was anything he could find that might help her.

Chapter 7
Fear of Life

Devlin got in late due to the icy travel and had barely fallen asleep before it was time to get up again. Taking a quick shower, the only kind he took these days because otherwise he was reminded of Masha, he gulped down a cup of coffee, grabbed two bananas from the counter, and headed to the office.

This morning he saw one of his toughest clients, a young man born with spina bifida who, as a result of his condition, was capable of erections but rarely ejaculations. On top of that he had the latex allergy so common to people like himself, so his first experiences with a condom had been disastrous. He was followed by a young woman who had been circumcised before being adopted from her native African home and experienced sexual discomfort as a result of scarring from that procedure. The third and final client before lunch was an intersex child and the child's parents who were struggling with what gender, if any, the child should choose as puberty loomed on the horizon.

After his appointments, Devlin met Mac at the club for a round of boxing in the dungeon, then joined him at a nearby restaurant for lunch. The day had turned bitterly cold, a mix of rain and snow was falling, but inside the fireplace crackled. The waitress brought hot coffee to both of them as soon as they sat down.

"Busy day?" Mac asked when they had ordered the chef's seafood special.

"Yeah, and it's not over yet," Devlin replied.

"Melissa?" Mac questioned.

"No, but she did call."

"I knew it!" His best friend all but crowed. "She's the one, brother. She's going to make you right again. I don't know how, but somehow it's gonna happen."

"Drink your coffee."

Mac just laughed.

Devlin finished his afternoon with an intake evaluation on a full mastectomy patient and a parole evaluation on a convicted rapist. He recommended that the latter never be allowed to see the light of day, but he understood the American justice system and expected his recommendation to be ignored. He could only do so much.

Still, if there was one thing that made his life worthwhile, it was his work. He liked that every case was different, that every day held new challenges. Devlin enjoyed helping people find happiness, especially in an area that many counselors and psychologists shied away from even though it was one of the most important areas in human relationships.

Melissa was his first and only client on Saturday morning. She arrived precisely at ten minutes before the scheduled time and sat primly on the edge of the seat he offered on the other side of the desk from him.

"Would you like to take off your gear?" he asked, indicating the long trench coat still covering her thin frame.

"No. Thank you."

Devlin sighed inwardly. He could help this woman, but only if she let him, and only if she met him halfway.

"Okay. But I'd like you to remove your hood."

"My hood?"

"Yes," he explained patiently, "I'd like to be able to look at you when I go over the treatment plan."

"Why?" she asked suspiciously.

"Because that's part of your treatment plan."

He didn't elaborate further. She had already been told that he was in charge of her care. It was time to test her resolve in this.

Hesitantly, she reached up and slid the hood off her forehead.

A shawl of golden blonde hair spilled out onto her shoulders. She tucked it behind her ears, sat up a little straighter, and looked directly at him.

"Thank you, Melissa."

"For what?" she asked, sounding perplexed.

"For doing as I asked. Now, are you ready to go over the treatment plan?"

"Yes. Sir."

Devlin explained to her that he would take a three-pronged approach to helping her. They would meet at his office every other week for counseling sessions. She worked as a hospital nutritionist so her weekends were free, and he expected her to volunteer every Saturday at the immigrant center where he got his first taste of selflessness as the second part of her treatment.

"Why?" she questioned. "What will that do for me?"

"It will help you get past your fear of strangers."

She seemed to mull that over in her head for a minute before nodding for him to continue.

"Now," he went on, "we have to work on your general anxiety and post-traumatic stress disorders. Before we can do that, I need you to make a list of everything that you are afraid of, every situation that you avoid. Be specific." He took a blank legal pad from his drawer and pushed it, with a pen, across the desk to her. "I'm going to get a cup of coffee while you get started," he explained, rising. "Would you like one?"

"Yes. Please." She didn't look up from the paper, still blank.

"Melissa."

"Yes?"

"Look at me when you speak to me."

She complied, blue eyes rising, nervous and puzzled at the same time.

"I will always expect this from you," he said. "Now tell me, how do you like your coffee?"

"Black. Three sugars."

Devlin's coffee pot was in the waiting area. He mixed his own cup, two creams and one sugar, before mixing her sweeter brew, remembering the first time Masha had made coffee in their cabin and almost flooded the place. They had mopped for an hour before getting it all up off the floor and still the smell greeted him every time he returned from work. To this day the smell of coffee reminded him of her. Shaking off the memory, he went back into the office to find Melissa laboring over the list, if her wrinkled forehead and teeth worrying her lower lip were anything to go by. Devlin placed the cup of coffee at her elbow before taking his own seat.

"Let me see what you have so far," he said, holding out his hand.

Reluctantly she passed the yellow legal pad to him.

She had written one word. Living.

"Well, it's a start, at least," he admitted, smiling to reassure her. "Now let's see if we can't elaborate."

The list ended up including crowds, new places, new faces, being trapped, being restrained, being touched, the dark, sleeping, not sleeping, not being able to understand what people were saying, being unable to trust her own judgment, being alone. He had her break these fears down even further so that they could come up with a hierarchy list and when that was done, he was surprised to find having her hair touched listed as the top fear.

"Better," Devlin remarked, setting the paper aside. "Now I'll explain the third prong in your treatment plan. It's going to be the biggest challenge."

"Okay," she said hesitantly, sitting up a little straighter and clutching the half empty coffee cup in her hand.

"We start with relaxation therapy. In the dark. If that works, we move on to imaginary situations, using the hierarchy you just gave me, and break your fears down into manageable parts. We work through each part, moving up the hierarchy until we get to the big ones. That includes the dark, as I said, touching, sex."

"Sex?" she squeaked.

Devlin simply nodded, waiting for her to process that information.

She looked away from him and he let her, knowing he had overwhelmed her, threatened her.

"With you?" she asked after a lengthy pause, making eye contact once more.

"If there were a man in your life, he could come with you."

"There is no man," she quickly interjected.

"Since there isn't, I can oversee your care and use someone else for that part of the therapy," Devlin finished.

She started to hyperventilate, which didn't surprise him, but he didn't believe in misleading clients about what they needed. Melissa hadn't had sex of any kind in over a decade, and before that what she had experienced was nonconsensual. Her former therapists had not been able to help her. If she was in a relationship, Devlin would be working with both partners and would not need to use a sexual surrogate, but since she didn't even date, that wasn't an option.

"I don't know," she finally admitted when her breathing was under control.

"It's not the usual treatment plan," he conceded, "but it is the best one for you. There is no rush, either. Everything will be done in small stages, and we'll adapt as we go based on your responses to what we do."

"Can I think about it?"

"You don't have to sign the treatment plan today," he said, "but you will have to sign it at your next appointment. It needs to be done before I can begin the relaxation therapy."

The breath whooshed out of her and she nodded, her posture relaxing fractionally.

"Okay." Devlin stood and grabbed his coat from the hook on the wall. "Let's get started."

They left the office and, driving in separate vehicles, made the quick trip to the Pilgrim Learning Center. There he introduced her to the co-directors before showing her into the recreation room where an elderly Cambodian man joined them.

"Mr. Chey, this is Melissa," Devlin said, using his hands to indicate who was who. "She is going to help you."

He directed Melissa to nod a greeting and to smile, then escorted her to a round table before long windows where she and the other man would work.

"What do I do?" she asked.

"You'll be playing board games," Devlin answered.

Her reaction was puzzling. While he would have expected her

to stiffen up at the idea of working alone with a man, he had not expected her to stiffen up at the idea of board games.

"Are you okay?" he asked, concerned.

"What type of games did you have in mind?" she questioned, her voice sounding pained.

"Monopoly. Candy Land. You know, things that help with counting and colors; simple vocabulary."

She nodded jerkily.

"And Scrabble. That's a great game for language skills."

He thought he saw her blanch.

"Melissa?"

She shook her head slightly, as if clearing it, and gasped, "I'm okay."

Despite her answer, Devlin stood on the other side of the room and watched her for several minutes to make sure she was all right before going into the office and visiting with the staff until her hour was done. Then he bid the staff goodbye, collected her from the rec room, and they left.

When they met again on Tuesday in his office, they talked about how Saturday had gone and why Saturday was important to her therapy.

"The center is a controlled social setting," he explained. "It's not a drop-in situation, so the people who go there are regulars."

Melissa nodded her understanding but made no comment.

"You put fear of not understanding what people are saying on your list," he went on, waiting for her to maintain steady eye contact before continuing, "If you spend time with others who can't understand everything people around them are saying, you'll confront that fear directly."

Again a non-committal response, a shrug this time.

"Melissa?" he prompted.

"What?" She looked confused, startled, as if she didn't know what he expected from her.

"Tell me how it went."

She was quiet for a few moments, then, "I liked Mr. Chey," she admitted as if surprised. "He's a nice man. I can tell that he loves his family and loves being in America."

"He does," Devlin agreed. "Wait till you meet the rest of them. Very bossy women; they nag the poor man like crazy. I think he likes the center because it gives him a break."

They shared a smile. Their first.

In the long morning session he could tell each time they got close to those fears most closely related to her rape and kidnapping because she would start looking away from him, start giving monosyllabic answers to his questions and those answers would get quieter and quieter. So Devlin moved away from those topics for the time being. Rather than directly attacking the source of her problems, they would start by directly attacking the results of them.

He asked her how she coped with things like crowds, new faces, and interactions with people in general. Melissa explained that she went to an all-girl undergraduate college and worked summers at a girls' camp. From there she went on to graduate school for nutrition, something that very few men studied, and when she finally got out into 'the real word' it was to take a job at a hospital. The number of people in a hospital kitchen was fairly small and in her role she wasn't part of the crew, so to speak, so she worked mostly in her office where the phone and the computer were her colleagues.

Devlin waited until she had finished with her summary before speaking. "Okay, you've told me how you deal with men, mostly, and only in an institutional setting. Now tell me about the other times."

"Other times?" she asked, those bright blue eyes round with confusion. "What other times?"

"You know, when someone takes an interest in you," he explained.

"Oh. You mean when they ask me out."

"We can start with that."

Devlin waited, watching as she screwed her face up in thought, and when the silence had stretched out, he prompted, "You're an attractive woman, Melissa —"

"I'm skinny," she interrupted. "And with my hair net on at work? Definitely not a pretty picture."

"Attractive," he affirmed, noting her discomfort at the idea.

He wasn't lying, though. She was thin, and tall, and from what he could see she was probably flat-chested, but for every type there was someone who liked that type. He had a fondness for thin women himself because they reminded him of Masha. That was also why he stayed away from them. Otherwise he would imagine that a woman was her. That her hair had changed. Or she had taken advantage of a plastic surgeon but that was her face under the mask she wore. Those kinds of delusions were dangerous to him and to the women. Because he saw her everywhere he went, he tended to avoid anyone that resembled her at all.

Melissa breathed out a heavy sigh. "I just say no," she told him.

"Just say no?"

"Yes. You know, like the drug campaign. I just say no. To everyone."

"That must be hard," he acknowledged.

"People talk about me. I know that they do. But I just say no to everything. To dates, to baby showers, bridal showers, weddings, all of it. I send gifts and tell them I'm busy."

"And how do people react to that?"

"The ones who tried fixing me up decided I was gay. So they tried fixing me up with women instead. Now they all just think I'm anti-social."

"That doesn't bother you?"

She shrugged.

"Melissa. Does that bother you?"

Another deep sigh. "Not at first. At first it was just easier, and I thought that eventually I'd be able to, you know, have a relationship. If I just got some counseling. If I met the right person."

"And now?" he prompted when she went silent.

"Now it's been five years since I finished graduate school and I live like a nun. But I'm not Catholic." She smiled self-deprecatingly. Devlin wondered if she knew that when her thoughts turned inward her speech changed and the slightest hint of southern accent emerged from what was otherwise a pattern worthy of a radio host, with no discernible vocal prominence to identify where she came from.

"Now it's harder," she admitted. "It was hard at first, telling people no, but now they expect it from me."

"And you would like to change that?"

"I don't want to be afraid all the time," she confessed in a very small voice. "I don't want to be alone all my life. I just don't know how to get over it."

"It's okay," Devlin told her, watching as bright blue eyes met his. "That's why you reached out to Lexie. You wouldn't have spoken to her if you hadn't wanted help."

"I guess."

"So let me help you."

He went over the treatment plan with her and Melissa signed it. They set up a series of future appointments, both at his office and at the immigrant center, and finally he worked through some deep breathing exercises with her in preparation for their next session. It would be on Friday night in the therapy room.

In the dark.

Chapter 8

Looking for the Light

Melissa sat in the middle of the room in a straight-backed chair, hands folded in her lap and eyes focused ahead, as instructed. Devlin flipped the light switch by the door, throwing them into complete darkness. He didn't move. Instead he listened to her. What he heard was rapid and shallow thoracic breathing, a sign of increased anxiety. He moved closer, but still behind her, and used the power of his voice to calm her. It was a low, gravelly voice unrecognizable to those who knew him before the accident thirteen years ago, but with a new tone that even babies found soothing.

"Deep, Melissa." She drew in a large gasp of air, held it briefly, then let it out slowly. "Good. Again."

When she had done the same thing a few times, he praised her. "That's it; very good. There is nothing here that will hurt you."

She made a small sound of distress but continued to take deep breaths.

Devlin came around in front of her, though she couldn't see him, and with the aid of a small pocket laser he moved to the table set up with the therapy light.

"In a minute I'm going to turn on the light. It will blink rapidly and you are to look into it. Keep taking deep breaths and concentrate only on the light. Okay?"

"Yes," she agreed.

He made sure that he was off to the side so that she wouldn't see him and be distracted when he turned the knob to activate the device. It shone directly into her face, blinding her to everything else, and he watched as she did what she had been told, concentrating on it.

He watched as her breathing rate slowed, waited for her posture to relax before saying softly, "Remember. Remember so you can forget."

Melissa tensed briefly, minutely, before settling into the chair again, her shoulders dropping, her hands falling open on her lap. Her head leaned slightly to one side. Her blonde hair slipped out from where it was tucked behind her ear and she didn't even notice. She looked boneless, like a child, and Devlin was glad that he could do this for her.

For twenty minutes he watched her sitting there, staring into the blinking light. He had seen Eye Movement Desensitization and Reprocessing work quickly on people before, but rarely in a case like Melissa. Those that responded to the treatment in a session or two were usually recovering from a single event instead of a complex situation like hers and she would need additional sessions.

When it was time to end this first therapy, he kept his voice low so as not to startle her.

"Melissa, I'm going to slow the light down now, then I'm going to count down to turning it off. Okay?"

"Yes," she answered, sounding drowsy.

"Good." He adjusted the controls and gradually reduced the speed of the blinking, watching her eyelids droop heavily over her eyes, noting the softening of her mouth and the slackness of her jaw. "Ten. Nine." She actually yawned. "Eight. Seven. Six." He dimmed the light further. "Five. Four." She was sagging in the chair. "Three. Two."

On the count of 'One' the room fell into darkness. Devlin listened closely, hearing only slow, steady breathing. He moved away from the table and came to stand in front of the chair, using spatial intelligence to find it.

"Melissa?" he said softly.

"Hmm?"

"It's time to go now."

"Okay." She nodded but made no move to get up out of the chair.

"Let me help you to your feet."

Finding the back of the chair, he ran his hand around it to her shoulder and helped her rise, then took a few steps back. He switched on the dim light over the vanity in the connecting bathroom before making his way to the office door. "I will be waiting right outside for you," he assured her.

Silence was her only response.

A few minutes later she joined him in the main room, lit only by one small table lamp. She donned her jacket, he set the alarm code, and they stepped out into the night, ending their first evening session.

Devlin thought of Melissa during the week. That wasn't unusual in and of itself, because he often thought of clients, their problems, and how he could better help them, especially those with complicated histories. Melissa was complicated. She had shared only part of what had happened to her, he knew, and that was also not unusual. Real trust took time. All that was required for now was her belief that he was a professional capable of providing the best therapy to meet her needs. Eventually he hoped that their relationship would develop to the point where she trusted him with all the details of her rape and captivity, but he accepted that it might never happen. Some things could hide in the subconscious mind for years; some never came out of hiding.

Still he was surprised when she showed up early for Friday night's appointment. She told him that she had slept soundly after their last light therapy session, the first sound sleep she had experienced in years, and was hoping for the same result this time. She went into the therapy room without hesitation and took a seat in the straight-backed chair to wait for him. Devlin wasn't fooled, though. Therapy could be a lot like having a shot; you knew it was good for you, knew that you would be better off for having it, but it was going to hurt and you couldn't predict exactly when the pain was going to hit you.

He moved quietly about the room getting everything ready. Asked about her week, listened to her answers, explained what he was doing at this session that would be different from the last, and when she nodded her understanding, he turned off the overhead light.

Again he stood out of sight and used his voice to prepare her for what was coming. Again he had to help her get control of her breathing before turning the therapy light on, but even with the changes planned it took a little less time this week than it had the week before.

This time he had arranged a straight-backed chair for himself directly behind her own. Once the light was on and her breathing under control, he took his place on that chair.

"I'm going to stay here during your session, Melissa," he informed her, keeping his voice low, soothing. "You will keep looking at the light, but now you will hear my breathing, smell my body, feel my heat."

She took a quick gasp of air and jerked slightly but didn't turn around.

"Good," he acknowledged. "I know this is hard for you, but all you have to do is sit there, just like last week. You have nothing to worry about. I'm here and I'm in control. You're safe."

It was a few minutes before she relaxed again enough for her breathing to even out. He watched her while he waited. He noticed the way her shoulders were the first to lose tension, how her elbows dropped when that happened, how the movement lengthened her neck. When that happened the light filtered through her hair on the left side and he noted an earring dangling there. No mate graced her right lobe. He wondered if it held some special significance. Because it rotated with every little movement of her body and because the light was still limited, he couldn't see what it was.

Her hands fell open on her lap when she reached the deepest level of relaxation. Her posture remained upright, and a less astute person might have thought she was not making any progress, but Devlin was a master at reading body language. For Melissa, given her background of being held captive and hurt, the open hands were significant.

Devlin remained conscious of his own breathing and movements as well. He made sure that every intake and exhalation of air from his body was measured and even. He was careful not to move so there were no rustlings of clothing to distract her from the light. Just the knowledge that he was present, that she wasn't alone, that she was in a vulnerable position and still had nothing to fear.

He kept the light on for a few additional minutes to let that relaxation take hold, sink in.

"I'm going to get up now," he told her, slowly rising from his chair. "All you have to do is sit there. Keep looking into the light." He moved off to the side and through the shadows toward the device. "It will slow down like it did before. Ten. Nine." He adjusted the speed and the dimmer. "Eight. Seven. Six. You should be very proud of yourself, Melissa. Five. Four. Tonight I asked a lot of you, letting me sit at your back, being that close to you. Three. When the light goes off, I want you to keep breathing deeply. Two. One."

Darkness. Silence. Not uncomfortable, or scary, or awkward. Just completely still with two sets of lungs at work and two hearts beating in the same room. Devlin approached her where she sat and crouched before her.

"I'm going to help you up again," he soothed, this week running his hands up the legs of the chair until he reached her lap. "I'm going to take your hands," he informed her even as he took the open palms in his own and rose, bringing her up with him.

He guided her to the closed sofa bed at the side of the room and after she had taken a seat, he came down next to her. "I want you to be comfortable, Melissa."

She murmured something indistinctly.

"You can't be comfortable dressed like this."

The silence that followed was wary, had lost its harmony.

Devlin waited. Patience was a virtue understood by few.

"What do you want?" she finally whispered, the catch in her voice touching him.

"Nothing drastic," he reassured her. She had arrived wearing a baggy sweatshirt and thick denim jeans that were not broken in yet. "I want you to wear something comfortable next time. Something you would have on if you were home alone, with no one to see you."

She made no response.

"This sweatshirt, these jeans, I think that you use them as armor."

She jerked a little and he imagined that if the lights were on, he would have seen her shake her head at the suggestion.

"I want you to drop your armor," he said softly. Then he squeezed her hands lightly in his own and, not wanting to scare her away or undo the progress made tonight, added, "Just think about it."

He thought of her again during the week, but found his thoughts of Melissa were no longer entirely professional. When he should have been remembering expressions on her face that indicated her feelings, he was instead remembering the way her blonde hair had a tendency to fall forward and roll against her shoulders when she relaxed and how she would tuck it back behind her ears. He was picturing the way she curled her hands in her lap when she was pondering an answer to a question and the way her fingers unfurled when she let her guard down.

It was just the similarities to Masha, he knew. He had experienced this problem before, seeing expressions or movements in other women that reminded him of her when there was really nothing to be seen. Just his subconscious at work, looking for the one person he was unlikely to ever encounter again and the one he needed most to find. He would have to be vigilant with himself. Keep his imagination in check and his client's needs the only priority. So when the co-directors told him that she arrived on Saturdays exactly ten minutes before expected and spent her hour playing rummy and Chutes and Ladders with Mr. Chey, he told them to make sure she played Scrabble the next time. It was one small way of re-asserting his professionalism.

"Professionalism? What are you talking about, Dev?" Mac asked. They were out for dinner on Monday night, had already finished their appetizers and were waiting for the entrées to be delivered, but Devlin had been staring off into space, not talking and now he was talking to himself.

"What?" Devlin replied.

"You're off somewhere else. Memories?"

"What?" Devlin shook his head, forcing himself to pay attention. "No. I was just thinking of someone."

"I knew it," Mac crowed, a broad smile spreading across his face that made Devlin want to hit him.

"You don't know anything," Devlin automatically denied.

"Then talk to me."

Devlin let out a sigh. Unlike himself, Mac had grown up in a loving home and come into foster care only when his grandparents died and there was no one else to claim him. They had raised him to always look out for and protect those he loved, no matter what, so when Mac decided to help someone, he was like a dog with a bone, and no amount of resistance could keep him from following his quest. Devlin appreciated Mac for that refusal to give up even if it was annoying at the same time.

"Come on, brother," Mac urged. "You know you want to."

Devlin had to smile in spite of himself, the good side of his face lifting while the skin on the damaged side simply stretched more tautly across the rebuilt bone structure beneath.

"You're a pain in the ass," he accused.

"But you love me anyway."

Devlin rolled his eyes at that. They both knew it was true. The feeling was mutual, and if there was anyone he could trust, it was Mac.

"All right, I'll tell you," he agreed. "But I don't want to hear 'I told you so' and don't go making more out of this than it really is."

Their entrees arrived at that moment. While the waitress was serving them, Devlin analyzed his thoughts in preparation for the conversation to come.

The waitress walked away, Mac took a bite of asparagus, chewed and swallowed, then said, again, "Talk to me, brother."

"I'm not sure what to say. Melissa is complicated. I can't give you any details, of course, but what happened to her is a lot like what happened to Masha."

"So you're trying to help Masha by helping her."

It would be easy to say yes, but it wasn't as simple as that.

"To some extent," he admitted.

Mac took a slice of his New Zealand venison and waited for Devlin to continue.

"I wasn't watching Melissa and thinking of her."

Mac nodded encouragingly.

"I always think of her, of course. Every day. All day. But when I was helping Melissa last week, just for a few minutes I saw her, the woman before me, instead of the woman I love."

They fell into silence then. Mac, despite his probing questions and his cocksure attitude, knew when to speak and when to stay quiet.

Across the table Devlin was dealing with a host of conflicting emotions. Thinking of another woman, even for a few minutes, was disloyal to Masha. Having sex didn't count. Noticing how another woman moved or the gestures she made, except in the most clinical of ways, did matter because it was a betrayal of the one who held his heart.

They talked some more as the meal went on, but not about Melissa or about Masha. The waitress cleared their empty plates. Mac ordered Drambuie on the rocks and Devlin got an Irish coffee. He held the glass handle, the cream almost to his lips, when he found himself admitting, "I feel guilty."

Mac simply nodded.

That guilt was still with him when Melissa walked into his office for her Tuesday appointment. He couldn't let it show, though. She needed a completely consistent tone of voice and greeting from him or any trust gained so far would be lost, ruining her chances for recovery. So he rose from his seat, forced her to shake his hand and make eye contact, and greeted her exactly as he had done before. "Hello, Melissa. Please take a seat."

She did as instructed.

"Remove your jacket," he added.

More slowly she complied, revealing a very thick and baggy sweater beneath it. Devlin bit back his frustration.

"Melissa." He waited until he had her full attention. Unusually bright blue eyes met his own hesitantly. "The next time you come here I want you to wear something in your own size."

She blinked and frowned.

"Not too large. Not baggy," he elaborated. "Something that fits you and is not meant to hide you."

Her eyes darted away from his face.

"Look at me," he ordered, his voice stern.

That got an immediate response and an interesting one. Not only did she comply right away, but while her expression was fearful, her body leaned forward in her chair, toward him. She was trying to please him.

"Do you understand, Melissa?" he pushed.

"Yes, sir," she nodded, her southern background coming out in both the response and the unconscious accent.

"Good. Now, would you like some sweet black coffee?"

"Yes, please."

Their session that day was a mix of progression and regression. Devlin wanted Melissa to do as he said because it would help her, but he didn't want her being mindlessly obedient and he worried that she was getting there. She told her other therapists what they wanted to hear. Instead, he wanted to hear what she needed to say. So he pushed her. Hard. Instead of asking about her general feelings of helplessness, he asked for specific details of her abduction and captivity. When half an hour had passed, she had crushed the cup in her hand, and her knuckles were white; he still had nothing specific.

"Enough," he finally snapped, showing her his displeasure.

"What?" she asked, jerking a little.

"Enough of this," he went on. "You're lying to me by omission. I am going to ask you some very pointed questions and you are going to answer them honestly. Don't tell me what you think I want to hear."

"I won't," she assured him quickly. Too quickly.

"We'll see," he said doubtfully.

He shot the questions at her like bullets, in rapid-fire succession, giving her no time to do more than blurt out an immediate answer.

He did not allow her to prevaricate or expound on any of them. Did she remember the rape? The captivity? Was she tied? With what? How often? What was she tied to? Was she beaten? With what? How often? Why? How did he keep her compliant? Did he deprive of her of basic needs? Was she fed? Clothed? Allowed to go to the bathroom? Did he share her with others?

Only when she was wilting in the chair across from him did he stop.

The silence in the room was deafening. One minute he was all but assaulting her, letting her know that he was angry with her for being evasive, not letting her hide from the anger or avoid it, then in the next minute he was done.

He watched closely as expressive eyes telegraphed her every emotion. Confusion at what had just taken place. Shame that she had revealed so much. Doubt that this was going to help her. Then the tears came as the emotions overwhelmed her. She looked away from him and he let her. Devlin came around to her side of the desk and removed the broken coffee cup from her now lifeless hands. He threw it in the trash, then came back to lean against the desk before her and took her hands in his own. Devlin pulled her up against him. None of this back patting or shoulder rubbing reassurance, but full frontal contact and his arms wrapped around her tall, slim frame. She stiffened for only a moment before completely dissolving against him.

She did not cry elegantly. Devlin was unsurprised that when the dam broke, she sobbed loudly and without restraint. Years of anguish were behind it. Years of repression.

When the crying tapered off and her body became a heavy weight against his own, she sniffed and said, "I need to get up," though she made no move to do so.

"Whenever you're ready," he reassured her. "I'm not keeping you." To prove it he let his arms drop away from her.

"It's not that," she admitted. "My contact popped out and I need to put it back in."

Devlin smiled in spite of himself. This was progress, when something so mundane could be shared after something so profound. He gave her shoulder a squeeze and set her away from him, twisting to retrieve the tissue box from the desk behind him. When he turned back around, she was just taking her finger away from one eye.

"Better?" he asked.

"Yes, sir," she admitted sheepishly, and pleased him by making eye contact without being told to.

Chapter 9

Possession

Memories of Masha rode him hard that week. Maybe because Melissa's case triggered so many comparisons. Maybe because of guilt. Maybe because she was never far from his thoughts in the first place.

Every song he played was for her. Every dream he had was of her. Every breath he took carried the whisper of her name.

He had returned from the lodge armed only with a bottle of Tylenol. As he approached the cabin, he could hear soft cries from inside and knew that even a whole bottle of analgesic couldn't provide the comfort that she needed. He needed to get her out of the cabin.

There was no washing away what had happened. Devlin knew that from personal experience. There was no running away from what had happened. No amount of distance would be far enough. But she didn't have to stay where she had been raped, didn't have to sleep in the bed where it took place, didn't have to watch the same door and worry that it could open at any time to her rapist. Even if it was only for the weekend, he could spare her that.

He took her to the apartment in South Attleboro and locked her in his bedroom with a couple of Tylenol, some ice, and a television remote control. Then he went to a nearby pharmacy and got a doughnut, one of those inflatable seats with a hole in the center that mothers sometimes used after childbirth. He added some magazines, fuzzy slipper socks, and some candy.

When he returned to the apartment, his contacts were waiting for him and they had unlocked the bedroom door. Once again he found Masha huddled in the corner of a bed, this time darting her terrified hazel eyes between the two suits that stared back at her, probably wondering which of them would pounce first.

"Get out," he ordered them, despite the fact that they were his superiors. He even pointed to the open doorway and stood aside until they had followed the directive. Then, tossing his purchases onto the end of the bed, he left the room and closed the door behind him.

"What the hell do you think you're playing at, Mick?" the first one, the one who usually did most of the talking, demanded.

"What the hell is it to you, Martin?" Devlin snapped back. He stood in front of the door with his feet braced wide apart and his arms crossed over his chest.

"Look at you! You look like a guard dog, for chrissakes, protecting a bone. Who is this girl? And what is she doing here?"

Devlin could feel the hairs rise on the back of his neck at Masha being referred to as a bone. She was his woman! The thought almost rocked him back on his heels because he hadn't realized until just that moment how he felt about her.

"Get rid of her," his superior ordered.

"No."

"Mick, this is a safe house. You bring women here and they'll start asking questions, start talking about who you see."

"I won't be bringing any other women here."

"That's not the point. Any woman is a risk. You're putting the operation at risk. She'll blow your cover."

"She's part of my cover," he retorted.

"What's that supposed to mean?" the other man, Lewis, asked, then followed up before Devlin could answer. "Don't tell me she's one of the prost—"

Devlin punched him before the last word had finished leaving his mouth.

"Jesus!" Martin exclaimed, stepping between the two of them before his partner could retaliate or Devlin could continue. "Stop it. Both of you."

Devlin said nothing. There was blood in his eyes. Masha was no more a prostitute than this man's sister or daughter or mother was. She was a victim and he was not going to let anyone accuse her of anything else.

"This operation is blown. We need to get someone in there who can stay cool under pressure," Lewis said from behind his partner.

"Don't be stupid," Martin cautioned. "This guy's already deep into it. If we get someone else now, they'll be on to us." Turning back to Devlin, he asked, "Who is the woman?"

"A victim," Devlin snarled, glaring at the man he had punched when he said it. "She's a girl, not a woman, and she's one of the victims."

"What is she doing here?"

"She's mine," he stated, the very tone of his voice daring them to challenge his claim.

Both men gaped at him.

"The Czech told me to pick a woman," Devlin relented. "I picked her."

"Oh my God," Lewis breathed, shaking his head. "You do know you can't keep her, right?"

"Fuck you," Devlin retorted. Once again Martin had to step into the breach. "So you're supposed to do what, keep her for yourself? As your personal slave or something?"

Devlin shrugged. "He said I could do whatever I wanted with her. He was worried about me being alone, without a woman. So he told me to take one."

"So she really is part of your cover," Martin conceded.

Devlin merely nodded.

"This isn't good, Mick. She could get in the way. Or get hurt."

"She's already been hurt."

"You know what I mean. When the shit hits the fan, she could get hurt bad."

"I'll protect her."

"You're crazy," Lewis said. "Do you have any idea what can happen during a bust this big? You're not going to be able to watch out for one girl."

"I will," Devlin promised.

"You'll get her killed. Because you'll be thinking about her instead of the job you have to do."

"Then let me walk away," he shrugged. "She can come with me."

Martin gave him a long, hard look before saying, "You can't walk away. And when it's over, you can't keep her."

Devlin said nothing.

"She's a pawn, Mick. Nothing more. Nothing less. Don't you forget it."

Again Devlin said nothing.

"The only way you can really help her is to keep her close for now and let her go when the time comes."

Devlin relaxed his stance slightly. He didn't agree with that, but he had cooled down a little and knew what they wanted from him.

"Can you do that? Walk away when it's over?"

"I can do that," Devlin lied.

Lewis didn't believe him, he could tell. Martin didn't seem to, either, but was at least willing to give him the benefit of the doubt.

"Okay. Let's get your intel," Martin said, taking a seat at the table.

Back to business. He gave the report they needed before hurrying them on their way.

When he went back into the bedroom, he came to a complete stop.

Masha sat in the middle of the bed, scissors in hand, her long brown tresses scattered on the comforter all around her.

"What are you doing?" he asked, stunned.

Of course she couldn't speak English, but the message got through loud and clear anyway. With one hand, she reached up and grabbed a hank of hair, giving it a hard tug, then shook her head in the negative. No one was ever going to pull her hair again. He had done it. Kraus had done it. Apparently she equated her beautiful long hair with restraint and she had taken it upon herself to deprive others of the ability to use it against her.

He understood that need. Victims took control in any way they could. When they realized that they had no control, their emotions ran the gamut from abject terror to murderous rage and everything in between. They wondered how they had contributed to what happened to them and what they could have done differently. They blamed themselves for being a victim. There were nightmares, flashbacks, mood swings, and coping mechanisms that did more harm than good.

After the first rape, Devlin did anything he could to make sure his foster father never had access to him again. When staying close to his foster mother and the other children didn't work, when hiding from the man didn't work, he resorted to making himself "unattractive" to him. He stopped brushing his teeth. Stopped changing his underwear for days at a time. Picked at his skin until it bled. Worked at being dirty. It didn't matter. His appeal for his rapist lay in his helplessness, not his physical appearance. Rape wasn't about attraction; it was about power, control, possession and punishment.

Aware of her fragile state, Devlin cautiously approached the bed. Making no sudden moves, he sat on the edge of the mattress and held out a hand, palm up. His meaning was also clear.

Her hazel eyes were first wary, then filled with tears of defeat, then clear and defiant as she jerked her arm away from him, clutching the scissors. He simply reached behind her and snapped them out of her hand.

Devlin locked her in the bedroom again while he made another quick trip to the pharmacy. This time he returned with a hair cutting kit and, although he knew little about cosmetology, half an hour later the uneven ends of her first attempts at a change had been transformed to something that was relatively straight. Her thick hair came to rest halfway between her chin and clavicle bones. He combed them out for her, fluffing the ends a little, but when he showed her how she looked in a mirror, she immediately tucked her hair behind her ears on both sides. Oh, well, what did he really know about beauty anyway?

The afternoon was spent trying to make her comfortable. He blew up the doughnut and showed her how to use it. The ice from earlier had melted in the bag, so obviously she had no idea what it was for and he had to show her, an intimacy that she fought against but one that she finally had to accept after he manacled both her wrists with one hand and held her legs still with his thigh, giving her no choice. He also had to force the Tylenol down her throat, literally, by holding her nose until she swallowed. He couldn't blame her for not trusting him, but until he could redeem himself for his earlier behavior and until they could find a way to communicate with more than hand gestures, she was going to have to do what he told her to do.

Masha fell asleep before supper and slept through to morning, something he was grateful for. Not only would rest help her heal, but it gave him a reprieve from the hurt and accusation in her eyes.

He used the time to take care of a few things. The first order of business was calling an acquaintance from his childhood who could procure just about anything, legal or illegal, for the right price. Devlin listed his requirements and at eleven he met a runner in the pharmacy parking lot to complete his transaction.

At midnight he called Mac.

"Talk to me," his foster brother said.

"I'll make it short. I have a woman. Her name is Masha Wozny. Sixteen. From Ukraine. If anything happens to me, I need her taken care of."

"Are you in danger, brother?" Mac asked with concern.

"No. Not more than I have been from the beginning. But I don't want them to get their hands on her if the shit hits the fan. I'm going to put her real passport in a safe deposit box at the bank so you know what she looks like. I'll add you as a signer and send a second key to you so you can get it if you need to."

"Okay."

"She's very young, Mac."

His best friend said nothing.

"Scared." Devlin took a deep breath and braced himself. "She's been used badly."

"How badly?"

"Like we got used by that dirt bag who was supposed to act like a father."

Mac's silence was loud in his ears. "And now?" the other man finally asked. "What now?"

"Now I'm going to spend the rest of my life making it up to her," Devlin vowed.

He couldn't know that they would be forced apart just three months later.

Unable to find her, unable to live without her, unable to end his life despite trying to, the best he could do was dedicate himself to helping others. His practice specialized in helping people like her. People like Melissa.

Chapter 10
The Key

Melissa wore a long-sleeved top on Friday night. While not exactly form-fitting, it was the kind of shirt that hikers layered themselves with, made of a shiny synthetic material, and it flattered her small breasts and lean silhouette.

Despite the obvious courage on display, she was as nervous as he had ever seen her before. She kept crossing her arms over her body, hopping from stocking clad foot to stocking clad foot, and delaying the start of their therapy session with trivial questions. Had he been busy this week? Glad for a break in the weather? Or did he like spring? Maybe he liked cold weather? Would he like to see warm weather again?

"What I would like," Devlin finally answered firmly, "is for you to stop jumping at every little thing."

She stopped moving, but her eyes darted around frantically as her mind searched for some other method of delay.

"Melissa," he said, using the voice that she now understood meant he wanted her full attention. She gave it to him, but her brow creased with worry and her chest heaved with rapid, anxious breaths.

"You know that what we are doing is helping you, right?"

She nodded uncertainly.

Devlin let his exasperation show. "Are you, or are you not sleeping better?"

She nodded again.

"Is that a yes? Or is that a no?"

"Yes, sir," she admitted.

"Then you have nothing to worry about. There is no rush here. Just trust me and we'll gain a little more each week. Okay?"

She nodded again, then caught herself and rushed out, "Yes, sir."

"Melissa?"

"What?" she demanded. It was the first sign of real irritation to come from her and Devlin was elated. She trusted him to show her irritation; a sure sign of growing intimacy. He smiled his pleasure.

"What?" she asked again, made wary now by his reaction.

"I'm glad to see you," he said.

"Oh." Her posture relaxed, but she still didn't seem to know what to do with her hands, wrapping them awkwardly around her waist.

"Why don't you go into the therapy room and I'll join you in a minute," he suggested.

She spun around, throwing a, "Yes, sir," over her shoulder as she hurried away.

Devlin let her go. She had already braved a lot this evening, wasn't done yet, and as he had told her, there really was no rush. He waited until he saw her settle into the chair, then turned off the overhead light and stepped into the room.

His chair was again positioned behind her own. Once the room was plunged into darkness and the therapy light had her attention, he slid onto the seat behind her, then leaned forward so that when he spoke his breath stirred the hair near her ear.

"I'm going to add something new tonight," he explained, his voice calm and measured.

She tensed, but less than he would have expected.

"In a moment I will lean down and put my hand around your left ankle."

Her breathing amplified in the quiet room.

"I will replace my hand with a soft restraint, sort of like a hair scrunchie."

Melissa made a little mewling sound.

"You can get out of it at any time. It will hold your ankle to the chair leg but as soon as you lift the chair, it will slide off and you are free."

She panted.

"I will also put the key in your right hand. That gives you two paths to freedom. You will always have the key, Melissa; always have freedom."

She said nothing.

"Do you understand?" he pushed.

She nodded jerkily.

"Here is the key," he told her, sliding it onto her right palm. "Remember, you always hold the key, Melissa. You are doing this by choice and the choice will always be yours. I will never take the choice away from you."

She clutched at the key, wrapping her fingers around it.

Devlin waited several minutes before bending to her left ankle. He made sure that she heard and felt his movements so that when he snapped the padded cuff around her ankle and the chair leg, the only surprise was the tiny click of the lock.

He ran his hand up the side of her left leg as he came upright, sliding it across her thigh until he found her left hand. It was open in her lap, but the right one was closed around the key. He ran his thumb along her palm, gentle circular strokes meant to comfort her.

"How are you doing, Melissa?" he asked at her ear.

She exhaled audibly before saying, "Okay."

"Good. You're not alone. You're not at risk. Just keep looking into the light and let it work for you."

He stayed close behind her throughout the session. Making sure that she could feel his body heat and hear the sound of his breathing. He maintained his hold on her left hand and every few minutes he whispered words of reassurance at her ear.

As she relaxed, her hair slid out from behind its usual anchors and rolled onto her shoulders but her hands were not available to tuck it back out of the way. He liked her hair. It was thick and soft, cut simply at just below the shoulders, and it spread like a shawl around her when free to do so.

It bore a clean, fresh smell. Like the rest of her. Being this close to her body, Devlin was aware that no heavy perfume anointed her skin. When she exhaled, only the mildest of scents wafted up to him.

When she breathed, the sound was quiet, peaceful.

He liked being close to her and that bothered him. He didn't want to notice her scent or the softness of her skin or the way her head leaned slightly to the side when she was at ease. He didn't want to think about the natural gracefulness of her movements or the way her hands curled open on her lap when she was relaxed. He had to keep his observations professional if he was going to help her.

When their session came to a close, Devlin slid his hand carefully out of Melissa's gentle grasp and ran it up her arm, bringing it to rest against the nape of her neck.

"I'm going to turn off the light now, Melissa. You will stay where you are until I tell you to move."

She made no response. "Did you hear me?"

"Yes, sir," she answered drowsily.

Devlin crossed the room to the light and gradually slowed it down, dimming it before turning it off completely. He didn't move then, but listened. Her breathing was deep and slow. There was no panic over being shackled to a chair leg in the dark.

He returned to the seat behind her, put both hands on her shoulders, and leaning forward, said, "I want you to stand up, Melissa."

Bracing herself on the seat of the chair, she did as he asked.

"Good girl," he praised. "Now I want you to reach down and lift the chair so that the leg is raised and you can step out of the restraint."

"Oh!" she exclaimed softly, then admitted, "I forgot."

That statement gave Devlin a great deal of satisfaction as a therapist. It meant that the relaxation treatment was working and that her trust in him was growing even more than he had hoped.

He helped her to maintain her balance by lightly grasping her hips while she removed the chair leg. "Now step out of the restraint," he reminded her, again holding her as she did so, then sliding his left hand down her thigh, calf and ankle until he encountered the padded item. He ran it up the back of her leg, letting her know where it was and where he was, until he stood once more behind her. His right hand had remained at her hip the whole time but now he moved it down the length of her arm, folding open her fingers

and removing the key from her grasp.
  "Thank you for your trust, Melissa."

Chapter 11

Progress

The next morning dawned cold and miserable, the kind of day when people huddled next to their wood stoves and watched television while drinking something hot. Since Devlin had no wood stove and didn't particularly care for television, he went to the club.

A few years ago Mac had converted the old shipping and receiving room into a state of the art aquatics center. In addition to an Olympic sized pool with multiple lanes there were two recreational sized pools and a children's pool. Cedar lined the walls of the changing rooms, saunas and Jacuzzis were tucked into corners, and a juice bar served cold, healthy drinks from in front of a frosted window where an overhead door had once been.

Devlin swam for almost an hour, exercising both body and mind.

The session with Melissa was still bothering him. He had told Masha on their last night together that he would know her anywhere, even in the dark, and the darkness belonged to her because she was his light. Melissa was looking for the light herself. If he started confusing the two women, even in his head, he wouldn't be able to help her at all.

He punished himself for his thoughts by swimming lap after lap. He blocked out the sounds of the children taking lessons, the high school teams competing, and the water aerobics class in session. He forgot everything, past and present, at least for a while. That came to an end when he passed the Jacuzzi on his way to the showers and saw one of the physical therapists working with a young woman who was very gingerly trying to lower herself into the tub of swirling water.

It reminded him of Masha.

When she had finally woken the next morning, he fed her. At least he tried to, but she made it pretty clear with her wrinkled nose that bacon and eggs was not her idea of a good breakfast and only picked at the food. Once she had pushed the plate away, he led her into the bathroom. The tub was full of hot water and Epsom salts and when he turned on the jets, it swirled like a Jacuzzi.

Masha looked at it just as doubtfully as she had looked at the meal he offered.

"You, bath," he explained, gesturing for her to get up and step into the water.

"Ne," she said, shaking her head and crossing her arms over her chest.

"Ya," he corrected, having no idea if the word sounded like yes in Ukrainian, adding gestures again to make sure she understood.

She refused. Eventually Devlin had to haul her up off the toilet and, with one arm wrapped around her middle, undress her with the other. He knew that she was still hurting and tried to be as careful as possible, but she didn't make it easy with her eel-like moves, trying to slip between his arms by going boneless. He had to give her credit for being smart, though. While physically fighting him had done her no good, this method of defiance was far more effective. Several times he had to reposition his arms to hold her. By the time she was naked, he was almost ready to throw her into the tub and be done with her.

Almost.

He had lost control with her already and was determined not to do it again. She needed his help, even if she didn't know it or want it. For one thing she was tired and sore. On top of that, she was a foreigner in a strange land where she knew no one. If that weren't enough, she was at risk for being sold to the highest bidder and he would never let that happen.

So he grasped her around the waist, as gently as possible despite her flailing arms and legs, and moved her to the tub. She used her feet to brace herself against the wall and prevent him lowering her into the water. He used one leg to dislodge them and ended up falling into the hot tub, cracking his head against the porcelain back, and dragging them both under the surface.

She came up sputtering and he came up mad.

"Damn it, girl!" he roared at her, good intentions lost in the need to vent over the pain in his head.

She shrank away from him, hazel eyes wide with fright.

"You should be scared," he snarled, pulling himself out from beneath her and standing in the tub. He was fully clothed and drenched. While she watched with trepidation, he pulled his shirt off over his head, then unsnapped his jeans. She hid her face then against the rim of the tub and curled into herself, away from him. He ignored her and continued to undress. At least he had another pair of shoes, he thought as he tossed his out onto the bathroom floor. Then he shucked his jeans and boxers down to his ankles, stepped out of them one leg at a time, and finally stepped out of the tub altogether.

Masha looked up, startled by his exit.

Devlin glared at her. He grabbed a towel from the rack beside the tub and began rubbing himself dry, and all the while she watched him. She avoided looking below his waist and instead concentrated on his arms as they moved the towel over his body, tracing the tattoos on his biceps with her gaze.

"Seen enough?" he asked, wrapping the towel around his waist.

He grabbed a face cloth from the rack and threw it at her. Unfortunately, since it was light and dry, it merely floated onto the edge of the tub. "Bath," he said with frustration. "You. Bath." Then he stomped out of the room and left her to it.

When he came back a few minutes later she had finished in the tub and stood on the mat beside it, a towel wrapped around her body. Devlin gave her a miniature vocabulary lesson about items in the room, including the hair dryer and when she was finished with that he introduced her to the toothbrush he had picked up the night before.

She actually smiled at the sight of it. He didn't blame her. It was pink and white and sported a Barbie doll on the end of it, but it had either been that or a red one topped by a pro wrestler's face. The pharmacy was rearranging stock. Those had been the only choices available for sale at the time. Devlin handed her the tube of paste to use with it and stepped out into the main room.

Her bag was behind the couch. He rummaged through it, coming up with a pair of jeans and a sparkly pullover sweater as well as undergarments. When she stood in the bathroom doorway, he handed them to her, indicating that she should dress before coming out.

Once she rejoined him, Devlin motioned for her to sit on the couch where he took her left ankle in his hand, snapping the metal bracelet around it before she knew what it was or could make any objection. Of course, object she did. She raised her foot to see what he had done, tried repeatedly to pull the offensive piece of equipment off and when that didn't work, kicked her foot out over and over again to see if she could shake it off. She shrieked hysterically, grunted with effort then disappointment, and eventually settled into quiet sobs, her head resting on the back of the couch and her hand over her eyes in defeat.

Devlin used the opportunity to test the security bracelet. Masha wouldn't want any comfort he could offer at this time, anyway, so he made sure that the signal was working and that his handheld device was properly tracking her whereabouts by stepping out into the hall and walking the length of the floor, then returning to the apartment.

From now on he would always know where she was. If she ran, he would follow. If she was taken, he would find her. She was alone in the world, much like he had been as a child. Before Mac, he had no one; no one who cared if he was hurt or lonely or afraid. Until Mac, he had no one fighting in his corner. Even then, Mac was a child like himself and could only do so much, but Devlin was a man. He would make sure that no one ever hurt this girl again.

While she continued to cry softly into the upholstery of the furniture, he breathed a sigh of relief.

Devlin left the club and crossed the city to the immigrant center, a former elementary school that straddled two neighborhoods, a relic of Boston's forced integration days. Today it looked as sad as its history with an overcast sky breathing down on the shingled roof and an angry wind twisting the swings on the playground in what looked like a macabre dance.

The inside of the building was a complete contrast to the exterior. People were laughing and smiling, the lights were bright, the temperature warm, and wonderful smells were coming from the cafeteria kitchen. Devlin loved the place. What had begun as a reform project for a young man sliding into a life of crime had become a second home for Devlin. Not only did he still volunteer for special events, but he was also on the Board of Trustees, the only civic responsibility he held.

"Hey, Mr. O'Malley," one of the co-directors called out to him as he made his way down the main hall to the recreation room.

"Reba," he nodded, matching his stride to that of the portly Jamaican woman when she turned to walk with Devlin. "What's new?"

"Your girl ees coming along."

"Good."

"You here to check on her?"

"Yeah. Have you got her to play Scrabble yet?" he asked, scanning the recreation room that they had come to but seeing no sign of Melissa there. It was early, though.

"Scrabble, Dominoes, everything."

"What time is she due in today?"

"Due? She here. Een the kitchen, cooking up a storm, dat girl. I tell her she needs fat on her bones, I don' believe her when she say she cook every day, so she say she prove it to me. That girl can cook!" Reba laughed. "She can eat, too!"

Devlin crossed the recreation room to the adjoining cafeteria. Over the serving wall that separated it from the kitchen, he could see Melissa at work. She was surrounded by Mr. Chey and his family and looked like a giant in their company. He had forgotten how tall she was. What really struck him, though, was that she was smiling. Not a great big, plastered all over your face smile like Reba would wear, but a genuine smile of pleasure nonetheless.

He watched her for several moments from his stance in the doorway. She was enjoying herself. He enjoyed seeing it.

"Hey, O'Malley!" the other co-director shouted from the far corner of the room where the coffee urns were set up, and everyone stopped what they were doing to look at him, including Melissa and her entourage. So much for observation. Devlin waved to the man and went to join him.

"Otto," he greeted with a nod, reaching for a Styrofoam cup and pouring himself a cup of coffee. "How you doing today?"

"Good. Better to be in here than out there today. Brrr," the older man said, shaking his body to emphasize the raw cold the city was experiencing.

"Much nicer in here," Devlin admitted.

"Come to see your girl?"

"She's not my girl, but yes, I came to see how she's doing. Reba says she played Scrabble."

"Scrabble, yah," Otto Faust said, his native German slipping into the conversation for a moment. "Nice girl. Quiet. Hurt. We've seen that before, though. We told her all about how you used board games when you worked here as a teenager. That helped, I think."

Devlin was glad to hear it. Anything that would make Melissa feel more comfortable and get her past some of her fears was a good thing. This place was obviously working for her. He finished stirring his coffee and turned to lean against the wall where he could continue to watch her at work in the kitchen. She had come a long way in a very short time. He wasn't foolish enough to think that it was his doing. She had simply been ready. Nothing else could or would work for clients if they weren't in that place where they were willing to reach out for help, then accept help when it was offered.

"What are they making?" he asked Otto, nodding toward the group in the kitchen.

"Some kind of bread. She says this weekend is Orthodox Easter and they need Easter bread."

"Easter bread?" Devlin croaked, clearing his throat. Masha

Ann Ruby

loved bread. She thought breakfast should be bread, a fat roll of sausage, and a hot drink. He had taken her shopping that second day in South Attleboro and let her pick her own food, in part to make her forget the ankle bracelet and in part to keep her from starving. Among other things, she bought sausage, beets, pork fat, the ingredients for bread making, and coffee.

"She cooks it at the hospital for the patients each year," Otto explained, unaware of Devlin's reaction.

"Oh." Of course she did. Devlin gave himself a mental shake. He had to stop lapsing in and out of the past like this. Melissa was not Masha. She was thin, tucked her blond hair behind her ears, and cooked Easter bread. That was not a long list of similarities. He had to keep the two separate in his mind if he was going to provide the therapy Melissa needed.

"Want to go see?" Otto asked, indicating the kitchen with a wave of his hand.

"Sure."

The bread was being moved from the cooking pan to a serving tray when he and Otto leaned over the serving wall. It was a golden brown braid, topped with salt crystals, and thin slices of pork fat and diced garlic lined the outside of the tray. Devlin found himself taking a deep breath to keep his memories at bay. He knew that bread—korovai—and that pork fat—salo. Not only had Masha served it to him, but after they were separated and his accident forced him to stay in bed for weeks, he researched everything he could about Ukrainian culture.

"Hello, Mr. O'Malley," Melissa greeted, her face flushed from the heat of the kitchen, blue eyes bright beneath her finely arched eyebrows. Her hair was back in a net, but it looked right on her. Not unattractive as she thought. The kitchen was obviously her element.

"Would you like to join us?" she asked.

He didn't want to, but he did anyway, because to refuse would be to make her wonder about him and he needed her confidence in him and his abilities. Needed to be consistent and supportive with her. So he sat, ate korovai with salo, and drank coffee. In fact, he ate more than anyone else because the Cambodians were not loving the food despite their enthusiasm for sharing the kitchen with Melissa. "Heavy, heavy," they kept saying, patting their stomachs to indicate that the food did not feel comfortable inside them. Eventually they returned to the kitchen to find something more to their taste, Otto was called away to give a new immigrant an introduction to the center, and Devlin was left sitting at the long cafeteria table with only Melissa on the other side.

"I guess we should have made vegetables and noodles," she laughed.

"With lots of heat," he agreed, smiling, charmed by the sound of her laughter. It was the first time he had heard it and he was happy for her that she had reached that level of comfort with him and the people here.

She smiled back, then grew quiet, eventually turning her attention to the sweet black brew in her Styrofoam cup.

"Melissa?" he questioned.

"May I ask you something, Mr. O'Malley?"

"Sure."

She looked up, giving him her full attention. "What happened to the side of your face, to your throat?"

The question wasn't that unusual. Some clients asked, some just looked at his scars and wondered where they came from. He preferred the direct question over silent speculation, but he didn't just volunteer the story.

"If you'd rather not tell me," she began apologetically.

"No. It's okay," he assured her, and relayed his tale.

It had been about six weeks after they took Masha away. She was living in Connecticut with the Ukrainian ice skating group that made their home there. He had suggested it as a good place for her to hide before the trial took place. He could also keep an eye on her there. No direct contact, since that was forbidden, but he could park at the rink and watch her come and go. Once, he thought she saw him. The sun had been shining on his windshield, so he couldn't be certain, but she had hesitated in the middle of the parking lot, then taken a couple of steps in his direction before her security detail had closed in on her. They ushered her to a waiting vehicle and the next day his supervisors raked him over the coals for his ongoing surveillance. They warned him that he could give away her location and put her at risk. He knew that, but he couldn't help himself. He needed to see her even if he never spoke to her; needed to know that she was alive. So when he made another trip to Connecticut just two days later, he was put on suspension and Masha was moved to an undisclosed location.

Devlin didn't share any of this with Melissa, though. Instead he gave her the shortened version. How the end of an intense relationship had devastated him emotionally and threatened his sanity to the point that he had tried to end his own life.

"How did you do it?" she asked when he paused, lost in the memories.

"I took the car I bought just out of college, a little red Mustang, and drove it through a Big Dig barricade."

"The long road project?"

"Yeah," he nodded. "There was nothing on the other side of the barricade and I knew it. The car plunged over the bank where a bridge had been and smashed into the road below."

He remembered it like yesterday, even though it had been thirteen years. The sound of the impact came so fast that he barely heard anything, yet in his recollection it was loud. Screeching metal, his body thrown forward into the windshield then back against the head rest, only to go forward again and embed his face in the broken glass. His leg snapped like a twig in multiple places and his foot was trapped beneath the pressure of the engine.

"The windshield wrecked my face."

"And your throat?"

Despite his wish to die, he had tried to call out for help and found himself unable to. "Crushed against the steering wheel. They had to do an emergency tracheotomy on the scene. The scars are from that."

"And your voice? Was it always gravelly like it is?"

"No. It changed after that." His lips turned up in a half smile. "I can sing, but I can't yell. No volume."

She was silent for a long time, absorbing what he had told her, then she surprised him by asking the question that few ever did, "And after that? Did you try again?"

Devlin didn't answer but instead unlaced the leather gauntlets at his wrists, laying bare the scarred flesh beneath for her to see.

Again she surprised him by leaning forward and running her fingers along the path that the knife had taken. She squeezed his palms once, offering comfort or sympathy, then sat back in her seat while he secured the cuffs once more.

"Was that the last time?" she asked.

"Yes."

"What made you finally stop?"

Mac. His foster brother had come to him in the hospital after the accident and wept at his bedside, yelling at him for trying to end his own life, then begging for his promise never to do anything that stupid again. It hadn't worked, though. Six weeks later Mac came home to his apartment and found Devlin leaning over the bathroom sink, both wrists slit.

"My best friend made me stop," he admitted to Melissa.

"How?" she questioned.

"He told me that he couldn't live without me, the same way that I couldn't live without the woman I loved. He said that if I took my life, he would take his own."

"And you believed him?"

"He doesn't say anything he doesn't mean."

"I'm glad," she told him with sincerity.

"Thanks."

"Is that when you decided to become a therapist? To help other people like you?"

"Mac said I should do something with that psychology degree collecting dust on the wall and the training that was wasting away in my brain."

"Sounds like a good guy."

"The best," he agreed, rising from his seat. "And if he's going to remain my best friend I'd better get going. He's throwing the annual company party tonight and I promised to make an appearance."

She rose from her seat as well and collected their empty Styrofoam cups.

"Don't forget that we're meeting on Tuesday this week," Devlin reminded her. He had to be in court the following week, so they were having back-to-back Tuesday sessions then would skip one before resuming their every other week schedule.

"Yes, sir," Melissa smiled.

Chapter 12
Funny Feelings

Mac knew how to throw a party, but tonight he had really outdone himself. When Devlin arrived, the black lampposts were glowing against the cold evening mist coming off the river. A young man in a coat over a tuxedo met him at the entrance to the parking lot and actually offered to park his Scout for him. Devlin tipped the kid but kept his retro vehicle to himself, his eyebrows raised at the extravagance. When he saw that a real red carpet had been rolled out over the steps to the main door, he wondered if Mac had made another million for them.

"What the hell is all this?" he demanded, when the man himself greeted him inside the lobby.

"A party," Mac answered. "Come on up."

They entered the antique elevator and Mariah, dressed to the nines, pushed the button on the console to send them up to the fourth floor. Mariah never worked weekends. Something was definitely up.

"This better not be about me," Devlin warned once they were riding in the car and out of earshot of anyone else.

"Don't be so vain," Mac laughed, cuffing him against the side of the head. "Who would want to party with you, anyway? You're no fun."

The car came to a stop at the fourth floor and they stepped out together. Devlin saw several people that he knew, all dressed up for the occasion. Wait-staff in black and white circulated with glasses of champagne and a three-piece jazz ensemble was set up in the corner playing something soft and mellow.

"Have a drink," Mac urged, nudging Devlin on the shoulder. "I've got one more guest to meet."

Devlin watched as his best friend rode the elevator back down to the main floor before turning to accept a glass of champagne from a server. Then he waded into the crowd and joined in a conversation about sports. The Celtics last game, the Bruins shot at a championship, opening day for the Red Sox, all were safe topics at a party and guaranteed to flush out everyone's opinions.

They were deep into the, "Remember Bobby Orr?" and "Curse of the Bambino" stories when Mac returned. He was accompanied by a young woman dressed in a bright green taffeta dress with black mesh underskirt, fishnet stockings and black ankle boots. Her generous bosom was barely contained by the bustier top. Above the swell of her breasts a black choker with a single diamond drop circled her neck. Her black hair was arranged into fat rolls that climbed on top of one another to add a good foot to her already impressive height. The two made their way over to where Devlin was standing and only then did he see past the garish outfit and recognize the woman.

"You!" he accused.

"Hello, dickhead," she sneered in response.

"Enough, you two," Mac intervened. "Dev, behave yourself tonight. Lexie, same goes for you."

"We're not children."

"Then don't act like it." Mac saw someone exiting the elevator and excused himself, leaving them alone together, only to return with Gremlin a moment later. Devlin greeted the tech, glad to see him again, surprised when the bespectacled young man slid his arm around Lexie's waist, looking up at her admiringly.

Devlin whistled low under his breath, eyebrows raised, and looked to Mac for explanation.

"Follow me," his best friend said. He moved over to the fresh fruit displayed at the base of an ice sculpture made in the shape of a woman. She had abundant curves and long skeins of hair.

"Venus?" Devlin inquired.

Mac nodded. "Beautiful, isn't she, brother?"

"Yeah," Devlin agreed, "A little too voluptuous for my tastes, though."

"She's perfect," Mac said softly, "just perfect. But maybe we can find something more to your tastes at the dinner table."

"Spill it first."

"Okay. It's about Lexie."

Devlin resisted a groan and Mac waited for him to control himself before continuing.

"You know I look on her like a little sister."

Devlin acknowledged that with a nod.

"So tonight I'm going to do the big brother thing."

"What's that?"

"Well, first I'm going to congratulate her on finishing her radiology tech program."

Devlin was impressed. He hadn't known that Lexie was going to school. "Wow," he said, because it was obvious that Mac was expecting him to say something.

"I'm not done yet," Mac said. "My second toast will also be to Lexie. I'm going to give my blessing to her recent engagement to Ernest Williams."

"Who is Ernest Williams?"

Mac's grin almost split his handsome face as he explained, "Gremlin."

"You son of a bitch," Devlin said with awe.

"Told you so," Mac smiled, pleased with his matchmaking efforts.

Devlin rolled his eyes at that.

"I could be right about you, too, you know."

"It's never gonna—"

"—happen," Mac finished for him. "Yeah, but that's what you said about those two."

"It still might not. How long have they known one another? Less than a month?" Devlin asked skeptically.

"No. As it turns out, thanks to you, brother, they discovered that they've known one another for a couple of years. They've been playing the same online games, just didn't know who the other one was."

At that moment the newly engaged couple joined them at the

table. Lexie fingered the diamond at her neck and looked squarely at Devlin. "Guess I owe you one," she admitted.

"Forget it," he said.

"You're still a dickhead, though."

Devlin actually smiled at that, and she smiled back at him.

Mac threw up his hands in exasperation.

Devlin found himself looking forward to Tuesday. His first client had female sexual dysfunction, something that affected about ten percent of the population. She was almost forty and had never experienced an orgasm. With his help, she was learning to masturbate in order to discover where her threshold was and how to climax. They had made enough progress that she was planning to go away with her boyfriend over the weekend and see what happened. For someone whose ex-husband had called her frigid and ruined her self-confidence as a result, this was a big step for her.

She was followed by one of his oldest clients, a transgender case named Gene and Genie. The victim of child molestation, adolescent rape, and abusive adult relationships, Genie would always need counseling. Their appointments were now down to once a month, though, and they greeted one another like old friends.

"How's your love life, doc?" Genie greeted with a smile, putting a plate of chocolate chip cookies on the desk for Devlin.

"Good, sweetie," he responded just as he always did, coming around to give her a big hug. "How about yourself?"

"Hold on, let me get to the couch," she teased, hurrying to the side of the room where Devlin did, indeed, have a chaise lounge for patients who wanted to use it. "Okay, now I'm ready to tell all. You ready, doc?"

"Any time you are."

The rest of the morning was spent doing paperwork, returning phone calls and emails. He had lunch delivered so that he could work on an article he was co-writing for a psychology journal. So engrossed was he in that work that he almost forgot why he had been looking forward to this day. Almost.

When Melissa arrived, she was not the same woman that he had talked with on Saturday. She was dressed in a lightweight black sweater that clung to her thin frame and she kept hunching over in her seat to hide her body. After ten minutes of watching her cower, he tossed his pen down on his desk and scowled at her.

"What?" she asked, startled by the action.

"Melissa, you're all but curling up in the chair across from me and you ask me *what*?"

She looked upset, guilt-ridden.

"I know I told you not to wear baggy clothing, but that didn't mean it had to be tight. What did you wear the sweater for if you were uncomfortable in it?"

"I'm not uncomfortable in it," she denied.

Devlin just raised his eyebrows.

"I'm not," she insisted. "It's just that, just that I'm not comfortable wearing it around you," she finished in a rush.

Now Devlin was surprised. *Proceed with caution*, he told himself. *Don't assume anything.*

"Why?" he asked, and the question lingered in the ensuing silence the way the echoes of a gong would have.

He watched as color rose in her high cheekbones, her blue eyes flickered, and she checked that her hair was tucked securely behind her right ear.

"Melissa?" he pressed softly.

The anguish on her face as she looked at him made him want to relent, but he couldn't help her unless she talked to him about what she was feeling.

"Tell me," he encouraged.

"You make me feel funny," she admitted shyly.

"Okay. Is that funny in a good way, or funny in a bad way?"

"I don't know," she answered. "Sometimes, you make me think of him."

"Him," Devlin stated. "Why don't we give him a name?"

She scrunched her face up like a child, brow wrinkled and lips drawn in, struggling to do as he wanted. "John," she finally rushed out.

"His name is John," Devlin repeated. "And what is it about me that reminds you of John?"

"I don't know," she said again. "Sometimes, it's like a look crosses your face, but that doesn't make any sense, because your face doesn't," she started to say, then gasped and covered her mouth, a look of horror on her face. "I'm so sorry."

"It's okay," he smiled, conscious that only one side of his face bore the expression while the other twisted awkwardly, sort of like the Joker but maybe not as scary. Or maybe even scarier, since he lacked the theater makeup the arch villain wore.

"I just meant that you couldn't make a look like him."

"Like John," he interrupted.

"Yes. Like John," she agreed, "but sometimes there is something about you that reminds me of him."

"And that makes you uncomfortable," he acknowledged. "But you don't know if it's good or bad?"

"It's not bad," she said, "it's just funny. I don't know how to describe it."

"Give it a try."

Her voice dropped to a barely audible level and her chin lowered as she went on, "It makes me feel jumpy. Like I can't sit still. One minute I want you to look at me and in the next I'm afraid you will. I don't know what to do with myself and it makes me feel funny."

Devlin sat back in his chair and looked at her. The poor girl really was a mess. He would call her a woman, but with her background experiences, she was still just a girl inside. If he hadn't thought so before, this conversation certainly proved it.

At length he asked, "Melissa, were you attracted to John?"

She jerked physically. Again color rose on her cheekbones and her face contorted.

"It's okay if you were. That still doesn't mean that what happened was your fault."

"He was good looking," she admitted.

"But that's not what I asked you. Just because someone is good looking doesn't mean that you find them attractive." He thought of his own disfigured features and how people were drawn to them.

"Did *you* find him attractive?"

It took a little while for her to answer. He could see that she was practicing her deep breathing techniques, trying to work up the courage to speak, so he wasn't surprised by the answer when it came. "Yes."

"At the beginning?" Devlin pushed, needing to get as much out of her as he could before she retreated again.

"Yes, but he made me nervous."

"Nervous, or funny like you said earlier?"

"Nervous."

Devlin just caught himself from saying the proverbial, 'I see', that therapists seemed to favor which could mean something or nothing at all and just aggravated the person in front of them.

"And how did you feel after the abduction? After the rape?"

Her lips trembled and her bright blue eyes filled with tears. "I hated him." A sob caught in her throat but she continued, "I was hurt. I hated him for that."

"Hurt physically? Or in some other way?"

"Both!" Devlin slid the box of tissues from the desk by his elbow across the surface to her and waited while she dabbed at her eyes with one. "I hated him for taking away my trust. He made me not want to ever trust anyone again. I was used like I wasn't important."

She looked away then, staring at the blinds that covered his window, profound sadness marking her features. Devlin sat still, watching her.

"Afterward, he was sorry," she said softly, still looking away. "I could tell that he was sorry. He tried to make it up to me, make me feel better."

When several minutes passed and she didn't continue, he questioned, "And did he make you feel better, Melissa?"

Blue eyes met his own at last. "Eventually."

"Did you find him attractive again?"

"Yes," she admitted sheepishly. "But not for a long time."

"How often, after you recovered from the rape, did you have sex with him?"

"I never said I did!" she protested.

Devlin nodded, not breaking eye contact, unrelenting, "But you did, didn't you?"

A mulish look came over her face and he almost laughed because it would have been funny in its childishness if this had been any other topic.

"How often?" he asked again.

"Not often," she said, grudgingly.

"Daily?"

"No!"

"Every other day?"

"No. If you must know, just one time before it was over."

Devlin smiled at her. "Thank you, Melissa. I know that was hard for you, and I appreciate your honesty. It's important if I'm going to help you."

"I didn't want to tell you."

"I know," he said reassuringly, "I can see that. But even if you 'agreed' to the sex that came later, it was still rape because he held you captive and you could not get away. Do you understand that?"

She looked doubtful.

"Just think it over."

She retreated in her chair, surprise on her face as she realized that she had leaned forward and taken on a slightly combative posture during that last line of questioning.

"Have you ever heard of transference, Melissa?" Devlin asked her now.

She shook her head in the negative.

"It's when a patient, or client as I prefer, experiences strong emotions for their therapists that they felt in another relationship."

"You mean you make me feel funny because he did."

"John."

"Because John did."

"It's possible. You found him attractive, and what you described earlier are the feelings of a young girl in her first stages of attraction. Since you didn't have the normal slow build-up to your first sexual experience, with flirting, and petting, and everything that goes with it, you wouldn't know what those feelings are like and that's probably why you're confused about your feelings for me. But they just might be your feelings for John."

"Maybe," she admitted skeptically.

"Again, it's just a possibility."

She shrugged noncommittally. Devlin smiled. He just loved tough nuts like her.

"Do you feel this way all the time, or just today?"

"It wasn't like this at first. I don't feel this way in the dark."

"What do you feel in the dark?" he probed.

She tilted her head to the side, thinking about her response, a look of concentration on her face, before coming out with her reply, "Safe."

Devlin was impressed by the certainty of her tone. "You feel safe in the dark?"

"Yes," she nodded. "When you're there, I feel safe. I'm not worried about what you'll do, even though I'm a little nervous, if that makes sense. I know that I'm safe."

"What about when I'm not there? What then?"

"Then I just pretend that you are. It relaxes me, and I feel safe again, then I can sleep even though I'm alone."

They both just sat there then, on opposite sides of the desk from one another, and considered her revelation. She was no longer conscious of what she was wearing. He was perplexed. Clients became dependent on their therapists. That was normal, but a good therapist was careful to make sure those feelings didn't develop to an unhealthy degree and he was worried that Melissa could go in that direction. At the same time, he was satisfied that she was no longer afraid of the dark and that she was sleeping. In fact, she looked much better than she had when they first met. The circles beneath her wide set eyes were almost gone. Her face, though thin, did not look gaunt, and she no longer held herself so tight that a loud noise might cause her to shatter. If their professional relationship ended tomorrow, at least he had given her that.

The sound of a door closing and a shuffle of feet from the waiting room disrupted the quiet between them.

"Sounds like your next appointment is here," she commented.

"Yes," he agreed, glancing at the clock, surprised that the hour had passed. He rose from the desk and walked to the exit door, one that led to a small anteroom so clients did not bump into one another. It was also equipped with a mirror in case one needed to freshen up before leaving.

"I'll see you on Friday night," he said as Melissa stepped over the portal.

Chapter 13
Letting Go

When she arrived for their evening session, she was clad in the frumpiest thing he had ever seen on a young woman; a corduroy dress that a first grade teacher might wear so that she had enough room in the skirt to sit cross-legged on the floor and still protect her modesty. "What is that?" he demanded.

"What?" she repeated, looking down at herself to see what he referred to, but coming up blank.

"That thing hanging on your body."

"A dress," she responded, as if it was obvious.

"You're not wearing that thing for our session."

"Why not?"

Devlin took her shoulders, commanding her attention.

"Melissa, the whole point here is to make you comfortable in your own skin, so that you can eventually enjoy sexual relations with someone you care about. Right?"

She nodded warily, still not sure where he was going with this.

"How can we progress toward that goal if you are trussed up in an outfit like that? You've got buttons all the way to your wrists and all the way up to your neck."

"Oh." She looked down at herself again, then back at him, "I wore it to work."

Devlin released her shoulders. "Well, you'll need to change out of it."

"Into what?"

"Good question. What do you wear to bed at night?"

Melissa hesitated, making him curious. He raised an eyebrow in her direction and color tinted her cheekbones.

"Never mind. Just go home and get into something comfortable." Devlin looked at his watch. "I'll give you fifteen minutes."

"Fifteen minutes!" she shrieked. "I can't get there and back in fifteen minutes if you expect me to change, too."

"Better hurry then."

He called the surrogate as soon as the door closed behind her.

Twenty minutes later she returned clad in a long trench coat, a determined look on her face, and walked right past him to the therapy room. When he entered it was to find the coat thrown over the sofa and Melissa seated in the chair wearing a t-shirt that barely covered the tops of her thighs. It had been washed and worn so many times he couldn't tell what color it was or if there had been any screen print on it. Her feet were clad in fuzzy slipper socks like you get at the hospital. Her posture was upright and her face bore the same mulish look he had seen in the office. Defiant.

Devlin smiled as he moved to the light switch. She would only be sassy if she trusted him. He liked it.

He set up the therapy lamp, then secured her ankle to the chair leg, not surprised when she tensed slightly in reaction.

"Just keep looking into the light, Melissa," he soothed, using the fingers of his left hand to feather over her ear, playing with the piece of jewelry that dangled there while his right hand slid across her palm on the opposite side, giving her the key to the ankle restraint. He listened to her breathing, alert to the slightest change. After only a slight hitch, she relaxed again.

"Very good," he praised, lowering his face until his lips were at the ear he had been playing with. "You're doing very well," he whispered.

She shivered. "Are you scared?" he asked.

"No," she answered softly.

"Just feels funny?" he questioned, using her description from earlier in the week.

Melissa nodded in response.

Devlin blew softly against her ear and she shivered again. With his right hand he could feel her thighs clenching. He decided to test the strength of her reaction, her willingness to accept his help.

"I think you're ready to be touched," he whispered, his right hand already moving out of her light grasp and down the side of her thigh, fingertips grazing across the skin almost to the knee then back again. Because her legs were so long, he was able to touch a lot of thigh beyond the chair seat. Again her thighs clenched, quivered.

"It's time," he told her, easing away from her body.

Melissa said nothing.

Devlin had to make sure that she understood. "The surrogate is here."

Even though he was no longer touching her, he could feel her tense.

"I'm not going anywhere."

She hesitated before asking, "You'll stay in the room?"

That wasn't how it usually worked. Melissa was an unusual case, though. Devlin considered her request thoughtfully, decided that she would probably panic and freeze up if he left her completely alone with a stranger, and made his decision. "I can if you need me to."

The air rushed out of her lungs even before she replied. "Yes, please." Then, as if she was making a confession, she added, "It's your voice that helps me. I need to hear your voice."

"Okay," he agreed, reaching forward to give her shoulder a reassuring squeeze before coming to his feet. He moved back and, staying out of her line of vision, said, "Just keep looking into the light."

Conferring with the sexual surrogate who had been waiting and observing from the doorway took only a moment, then the man was replacing him in the chair at Melissa's back. He leaned forward as Devlin had, breathed softly against the hair at the side of her neck, and ran his hand along her thigh just as Devlin had done.

The surrogate repeated the action, this time using both hands, touching both sides, his breath at her ear now, the jewelry spinning wildly in response and her body trembling in the chair.

For the first time in his professional life it bothered Devlin to watch. Normally, if he stayed in the room, he could remain clinically detached, but he found it bothered him to see the other man with his hands on Melissa.

The surrogate sat forward in his seat, this time running his hands to the backs of her knees. Her slender body bowed forward in reaction, her neck arching and her head thrown back. That put her earlobe within his reach and he took advantage of it. Flicking his tongue against it, once, he sucked the soft tissue into his mouth and repeated the caress at the back of her knees.

A soft mewling sound followed by light panting filled the air.

"The light," Devlin reminded her, his voice more guttural sounding than usual.

"I'm trying," she confessed.

"Having trouble?" Devlin asked, but before she could answer the surrogate moved his mouth from her earlobe to the side of her neck, softly biting the tendon there before laving the spot, and any reply she would have made was lost in the rush of breath that escaped her.

Devlin braced himself as the other man's hands continued to run up and down the backs of her thighs and knees, his mouth devoted to her ear, neck, and shoulder. She started to undulate in her chair. The surrogate doubled his efforts. Her breathing rose in volume and tempo. Devlin glanced at her face, saw that her eyes were half closed, and glanced down her body to see the outline of her raised nipples pressed against the worn fabric of the t-shirt.

The surrogate switched his mouth to her other ear and a shudder raced over her at the momentary loss of his attention. He nuzzled her hair aside and lapped at her corded neck. She tilted her head, giving him better access, and he nipped her earlobe, then suckled it between his lips.

Melissa was shaking from head to toe. Her legs quivered where the other man touched them. Her feet were rubbing against the chair legs, splaying her thighs apart in an unintentional but most inviting way. She rolled her head bonelessly on her shoulders, offering her neck and ear to him. Her torso bowed and swayed against the chair seat.

Anyone else would have thought she was more than ready for sex, but Devlin knew better. The woman was not going to go from 'funny feelings' to sex just like that.

"You've done very well, Melissa," Devlin said softly.

The surrogate slowed the stroking of his hands and reduced the ministrations of his mouth from an all out assault to a series of gentle kisses and occasional blowing.

"This was a good start."

Gradually Melissa settled back into her chair. Her breathing was ragged, her body filmed with a fine sheen of perspiration, but her movements stilled except for the occasional shiver. The surrogate eased his hands up to her shoulders, rose from his seat and kissed the top of her head before silently leaving the room.

Devlin was actually jealous of the man; was glad to see the surrogate go.

"I'm going to adjust the light now," he explained to Melissa before stepping away from his observation post. "Just keep looking at it."

As always, Devlin kept himself out of her line of vision while he slowed the speed of the blinking, dimmed the glare to a glow, and eventually turned off the therapy light.

The room fell silent. On stocking feet he made his way back to the chairs. Again he took her shoulders in his hands, but this time it was to help her to her feet where he instructed her to remove the chair leg from the restraint around her ankle. Having done that, she stepped out of the padded circlet and he took back the key.

He had to help her on with her shoes. Not because it was dark, but because her legs were weak beneath her and she swayed a little on her feet in the aftermath of the night's session. By the time her jacket was on and he held the front door for her she had regained her balance, but he almost lost his own equilibrium when he heard her say as she passed, "You almost make me forget him."

Back at his condo, Devlin thought about that last comment while strumming his guitar. She almost made him forget, too. When he was with Melissa he stopped wondering where Masha was, how Masha was, and whether or not he would ever see her again. Now if only Melissa had a daily therapy appointment, at least seven days of the seven-day week, he might actually move on with his life

Masha had remained angry with him until Kraus took them on a trip to Washington, D.C. the following week. The Czech explained that every now and then they needed to slow down their movements so that they didn't make anyone suspicious. When that happened, he would visit the clubs, treat himself to a little vacation.

So the three of them climbed into the front seat of the other man's SUV and headed South. Even though the vehicle had plenty of room, Masha pressed against his side to avoid any contact with Kraus. Devlin couldn't blame her. He wrapped his arm around her shoulder and held her close, angling his body so that his shoulders were wedged against the window to give her even more room.

It was a long drive to the capitol. They stopped at a couple of rest areas on I-95 where he made Masha share the handicapped rest room with him so that she wouldn't run away or be subjected to time alone with Kraus, then they walked a little, stretching their stiff muscles. By the time they arrived at the suburban development that was their destination, Masha was asleep and he was exhausted.

"Baby," he said as he removed their seat belts, sliding out from beneath her where she rested against him. Her head lolled against the padded rest, but she didn't wake.

"Masha, baby," he called again, a little louder. When that got no reaction, he slid one hand behind her back, the other beneath her thighs, snagged their overnight bag with his fingers from behind the seat and lifted her out of the car.

She woke then. Startled, her immediate reaction was to jerk back and almost unbalance both of them, which had her gasping and clutching at his shoulders.

"It's okay," he reassured her, giving her a squeeze.

"You spoil her," Kraus commented as they waited at the door for someone to answer the bell.

Devlin glared at the back of Kraus's head. He hated this man. While it had been easy enough to hide his feelings before Masha, he was now finding it a real challenge.

"Ah! My friend, Kraus!" a booming voice greeted as the door swung open. A wiry man in his late twenties or early thirties with close-cropped dark hair and a long mustache stood aside, smiling at them. "Come in! Come in!"

The house was everything you would expect from its exterior. Middle class, comfortable furnishings, center staircase covered in deep pile carpeting, the kind of place where you would expect to see Mom, Dad, and the kids at the dinner table. Instead, the only other occupant was a big guy at the breakfast bar, all in black, greasy looking, and with a cigarette drooping from his thick lips while his eyes narrowed at the sight of them. Devlin lowered Masha's feet to the floor but held on tight to her.

"Vigor, say hello to Kraus!" their host ordered.

"Hello, Kraus," the flat voice obeyed.

"And who are your friends, Kraus?"

"This is Mick," Kraus introduced, "he works with me at the camp. Very good with documents, passports, stuff like that. Mick, my friend Anton."

"And this?" the little man asked, ignoring the introduction to circle around Devlin and inspect Masha. "Who is this?" he asked with interest.

"She's mine," Devlin asserted fiercely, blood in his eyes.

"Relax, Mick," Kraus admonished, slapping him on the back and moving to take a stool beside Vigor. "You can't blame Anton for looking. It's his business."

Anton shrugged. "She could make a lot of money for me, but I get it. She's yours. When you get tired of her, you send her my way."

Masha was trembling at his side. She was not a stupid girl and she knew very well what type of men she was looking at. Men like Kraus. If Devlin had any choice, he would take her out of this house and out of their sight, but he was doing a job and couldn't blow his cover, so instead he asked if there was a place where they could put their stuff down and take a shower.

They were shown to a bedroom on the second floor with an adjoining bath. As soon as they were inside Devlin locked the door behind him and pushed one of the tufted armchairs up against it. Masha's eyes widened, but she remained silent. He put their bag on the end of the bed, unzipped it and pulled out a spare set of clothing before leading her into the bath where they both relieved themselves and changed. He would have liked a shower after the long drive, but he didn't want to be naked in this house or in any other way vulnerable.

Returning downstairs they joined the others in the attached garage where Anton sat behind the wheel of a mini-van. Vigor was in the passenger seat and Kraus took the back. That left Devlin and Masha to share the two seats in the middle row. *Between ugly and evil*, Devlin thought, holding Masha's hand.

They drove into the city to a club that looked inconspicuous enough from the outside. Brownstone exterior, iron grilled banisters, and mullioned windows made it look almost like a respectable business, but the curvy sign at the door showing two dancing girls entwined around the same pole advertised the establishment for what it was. That and the big bouncer who stopped them at the door with a beefy hand in the middle of Devlin's chest.

"They're with us," Anton explained, waving the bouncer back.

The big man stepped aside, but when Masha moved to go past him, he said, "Too young," and detained her with a grip on her upper arm.

"Get your fucking hands off my woman," Devlin snarled, wedging his body between her and the bouncer, not caring that the man was bigger and probably stronger than he was.

"Mick, relax," Kraus reprimanded.

"Your buddy has a problem," Anton warned, but to the bouncer he said, "She won't drink."

"We'll take care of her," Kraus added.

"I'll take care of her," Devlin clarified to the bouncer, backing off only after the other man did.

It was an awful place to take Masha. Businessmen, politicians and lobbyists sat at tables placed on both sides of three pole dancing areas. The girls were scantily clad and heavily tipped, if the money sticking out of their panties and garter belts was any indication. Devlin knew that none of that money was theirs, of course. All three of the girls on tonight had been processed through the Rhode Island camp. He remembered each face. They remembered him. He couldn't make eye contact with them so instead he concentrated on

Masha, who was physically buffeted by each swell of noise in the room, visibly shrinking from the interest of the men around them, trying her best to decide whether he represented safety or yet another threat to her well-being. Devlin pulled her out of her chair and onto his lap to reassure her.

When a uniformed police officer stopped to say hello to their companions, Masha straightened away from him momentarily, shaking like a leaf in a storm, then collapsed back against him. He understood. The officer should have represented a chance at escape, but seeing his familiarity with the others made it clear that there was no help to be found there.

Devlin looked around at the rest of the clientele. These were important people. People who would prosecute the scum he was with when enough evidence was brought to them; people who would change laws to prevent such crimes from happening again. Yet here they were enjoying the sight of these nubile young women, pinching them, touching them, tipping them, then leaving to sleep in their own comfortable beds without giving them a second thought.

When one of the dancers explained to a customer beside him that she was going to college, the man gave her a very large tip and Devlin didn't miss Vigor's pleased smile. None of that money was for college; none of it was even for the dancer. As soon as their fourteen hours was over, these girls would be transported back to an apartment and left for the night until they were needed for the lunch opening tomorrow. A nice apartment, of course, but not one they would dare to leave. Their handlers kept them compliant with threats, beatings, and rape as well as the fear of deportation. By this time they were probably convinced that no one would help them. Foreign girls, forged papers, limited English; they had little hope of anyone caring about their lot in life.

Devlin held Masha closer to him, glad that the fates had seen to it that he and this girl ended up together. He would protect her from a future like this. None of the girls deserved what had happened to them, but she was special.

"When I'm looking for the light, in the middle of the night," Devlin sang now in his gravelly voice.

He put his hand across the guitar strings, stilling the music, a profound sadness settling on his broad shoulders.

"Searching for the brightest star, there you are."

He didn't know what was bothering him. Was he starting to let Masha go, accepting that their paths were unlikely to ever cross again, and finally moving on? Would the memories start to fade, when for thirteen years they had been part of his everyday thoughts?

He often wondered if Masha had repressed her memories of their time together. Moved on with the aid of the witness protection program and a new name and started a life without him. Seen a counselor or counselors and told them all about him. About the rape, being tied up, being kept with him at all times so there was no privacy and no opportunity to escape. He hoped that whoever she saw had helped her reach the conclusion that after that first awful night, he was motivated not by a sense of ownership but by a desire to protect her from a fate worse than being shackled to him. He hoped all those things for her but despite his genuine wish for her to have a full, happy life, he hoped the people who helped her were female. He could not think of her with another man; not even a therapist.

"Hypocrite," he castigated himself as he hung the guitar back on the wall and slid the pick into the frets for safekeeping.

Chapter 14

Falling

Knowing that he was being contradictory and changing his feelings were two different things. In the morning Devlin got the tires rotated on the Scout, picked up a few things for the condo, then headed to the club. Mac was out so instead of the sparring match he was in the mood for he ran on the treadmill and used a rowing machine for a while.

On his way out he ran into Gremlin and Lexie. She wore stacked-heel black boots that made her tower over her fiancée, but the tech didn't seem to care. Both were smiling. Her expression faltered a little bit at the sight of him.

When she held her tongue, Devlin did the same. Maybe it was that attempt at civility or maybe it was his own complex emotions, but he didn't want to fight with her today. So he just nodded, said hello, and held the door for them as they went into the club and he left.

He drove to the immigrant center without a second thought for his motivations. He needed to see Melissa. Between his previous weekend visit, Tuesday's office session and last night's progress in systematic desensitization, they were on the verge of a breakthrough. If things continued at this rate, she would be well on her way to dating comfortably by the end of the summer. Devlin found he didn't like that idea as much as he should have so he pretended it hadn't crossed his mind, parked his Scout, and went into the building.

She was in the rec room playing Scrabble with Mr. Chey. From the doorway Devlin watched as the spring sunshine bathed her face, outlining her high cheekbones and small tipped nose, and filtering through the light blonde hair that had come loose from its mooring behind her ear. She was an attractive woman when she lost the pinched look of worry that often marred her lean features. Not the type that would attract a man like Mac, he knew, or even the average man, but his type. Masha had been lean in the way that teenage girls sometimes were, with coltishly long limbs and straight lines that had not yet matured to their roundest potential. Ever since then he had found himself drawn to lean lines.

"Mr. O'Malley! Back again, I see," Reba greeted, stopping in the hall with a pushcart of clean linens.

"Yeah. Thought I'd stop in and see how she is outside of the kitchen."

"She's a nice lady," Reba said, nodding her head for emphasis before trundling on down the hall with her load.

Devlin pushed himself away from the door frame and crossed the rec room to where Melissa sat. She saw him almost right away and he watched with interest as she reached for a shrug on the seat beside her, then changed her mind and did her best to sit up straight in the blouse she wore. It wasn't form fitting, but it was flattering, the satin material showing off her slender figure and the dusky rose color bringing out the matching tint of her cheeks and the blue in her eyes. She couldn't resist tucking her fallen hair back, but that was a small thing. Melissa facing him directly and not covering her body self-consciously was a big thing.

"Hello, Melissa," he greeted, taking a seat between she and the elderly Cambodian, "Mr. Chey."

"Mr. O'Malley," they spoke almost in unison.

"Do you have room for a third?"

For an answer, Mr. Chey handed him a wooden rack and Melissa dealt seven lettered tiles for him to place on it.

He stayed and played with them for an hour. Devlin had learned to use games, both board and other types, to teach new immigrants the English language when he came here as a teen. It was that experience that helped him tutor Masha. The first thing he did when they were left to their own devices on the second day in D.C. was take her shopping. They bought flash cards, board games, and CDs for children. The sooner she learned English, the safer she would be.

"Mr. O'Malley?" Melissa asked, and Devlin became aware that he was staring blindly at the table while she packed up the Scrabble game.

"Sorry," he apologized. "Where did Mr. Chey go?"

"With his wife," she said, laughing softly, "I think that after last weekend she decided that he would get fat from my food so she's going to take him home for lunch."

"I see," Devlin smiled, sharing her humor. "Will they be back?"

"No. I think one of his kids is getting married, or divorced, or something," she shrugged her shoulders with another laugh, "I couldn't follow exactly what he was saying."

"You're doing a great job, though. Both of the co-directors say so."

"Well, they would have to, wouldn't they? You're on their Board of Directors."

"Caught that, did you?" He shrugged it off. "Believe me, they would still tell me the truth. Besides, I can see for myself that you're doing well. Establishing relationships with people who were strangers. Communicating with someone you can't always understand."

She thought about what he said for a few minutes, eyes down, running her hands along the seams of the Scrabble box top. When she looked up at him, her eyes were steady, her voice reflective. "You really are very good at what you do, Mr. O'Malley."

"Thanks," he said, touched by her sincerity.

They experienced a slightly awkward pause, then Melissa rose, game box in hand. "I've got to put this back in the closet," she explained.

"Of course. I'd like to talk to you about something when you're done."

"Okay."

He watched her walk away, knowing that she was conscious of his appraisal. She carried herself well, posture straight and movements graceful, unlike some tall people who tried to blend in with those around them and hunched to achieve their goal. Devlin was tall himself, so he saw no reason to do so, but he knew a lot of women who did.

When she walked back toward him, he again admired the way

she moved and the way her outfit complemented her form. The rose blouse was worn over a round-necked black top, both tucked into black dress pants that flared at the bottom. A small silver buckle adorned the belt around her waist, and a silver hoop earring winked at him, but other than that she was without ornamentation. Lean and clean. He liked that.

She resumed her seat at the table and looked at him expectantly.

"Would you have lunch with me, Melissa?" he invited.

Her head went back a little in surprise. When he just sat, waiting for her answer, she asked, "Is this therapy or just lunch?"

"How about both?" he suggested. "I enjoyed talking with you last weekend and I need to eat. Do you?"

"Yes," she admitted honestly.

"Good. While we're eating, we can talk. You need more practice at intimate settings, so this will also help with that."

"Last night was intimate," she retorted, then gasped at what she had said and blushed to the roots of her hair.

Devlin smiled at her. "It was. Now let's practice intimacy of a different sort."

Another small hesitation and she accepted his invitation.

He picked a nearby pub known for hearty American food, thinking that would appeal to her, and he was right. They got a couple bottles of dark beer from a microbrewery on the Cape and shared a small loaf of homemade whole grain bread with butter while waiting for their meal.

"Tell me about your education," Devlin prompted, licking the butter from his lips and taking a swig of the beer.

"It was a little unusual," she said. "After the abduction, I was home-schooled."

When he made no comment, she continued.

"I always liked to cook, and I had a lot of time on my hands since I could get my class work done in a few hours, so I cooked. A lot."

"You do seem to enjoy it," he remarked.

"I do. I also like to eat a lot," she confessed.

"So they tell me." She shrugged apologetically, but continued. "So anyway, I learned to cook a lot of different types of foods. I especially like to bake, and my favorite thing is to cook holiday foods from around the world."

"That's how you knew about the Ukrainian Bread and Salt tradition," he observed.

"You know about it?" she asked, surprised.

"I've been coming to the immigrant center for a long time," he explained, though that wasn't where he got his knowledge of that particular culinary offering.

"Oh. Of course." She sliced off another piece of bread from their loaf and spread it with butter. No dieter's pat, but a liberal coat of the creamy stuff. "Well, when it was time to go to college, it just seemed natural to study food. I like to cook and I like science, so I picked a school with nutrition as a major, and that's what I studied."

"And that was down South?"

Her bright blue eyes went wide, her mouth forming an 'o'. "Why would you say that?"

"Every once in a while I hear a little southern drawl in your voice." That seemed to bother her. He wasn't sure why, maybe it was because she didn't want to stand out, so he went on. "It doesn't happen often. I probably notice it where other people wouldn't. You know, since I observe people's behavior for a living."

She nodded, looking relieved, and stopped talking to eat her bread. Devlin sat back in his chair and forced himself to look around, at the other diners, the bar patrons, the paintings on the wall. That way Melissa wouldn't feel self-conscious and he wouldn't give away his growing interest in her. Keep it professional, he told himself. So far he hadn't breached any ethical lines, and everything he was doing was helping her.

"What about your family?" he asked when she had finished and used the napkin to dab the crumbs from her mouth.

Her movements stilled, a great sadness washing over her features. "I sort of lost contact with them."

"You weren't living with them?" he probed.

She shook her head in the negative. "After the abduction I stayed with some people who offered to help me, and by the time I got in touch with my family, they had moved. I don't know where they are, or who is left."

"Couldn't you get a forwarding address?"

She shrugged, fiddling with her napkin ring, not looking at him.

"Were you afraid to face them, Melissa?" he asked quietly.

He didn't think she was going to answer, but after a moment she did, her voice filled with consternation and shame. "I was stupid. How could I tell them what had happened? It was my fault. I put myself in that situation."

Devlin reached across the table, stilling her hands where they were twisting the napkin ring. "Look at me, Melissa." He waited until bright blue eyes lifted to meet his gaze. "Were you an adult then?"

Looking puzzled, she shook her head in the negative.

"Right. You were a child."

"I was a teenager," she objected, as if that confirmed her guilt, explained why she should have known better.

"Melissa, small children are afraid of strangers. Not just because of their parents' warnings, but because they have an innate distrust of people they don't know unless their parents are with them. They have a radar that tells them when someone is bad. But teenagers lose that ability and they don't get it back until they're adults, sometimes not until their mid-twenties. That's why teenagers take risks that small children and grown-ups don't. It's why they are so often the victims of crime. Their judgment is off during those years."

"But I should have known better," she insisted.

"No, Melissa."

She looked as if she wanted to believe him but couldn't.

"I wouldn't tell you this if it wasn't true."

"Really?" she asked, skepticism evident in her voice.

"Really. You were a victim. Victims aren't responsible for the bad things that people do to them."

Their meals arrived then. Both had ordered the pot roast special and they weren't disappointed. They tucked into the meat and vegetables with gusto, neither saying anything until the plates were cleared away and the coffee had been ordered, one sweet and dark, the other light and mild.

"What about you?" Melissa asked, preempting his planned question for her.

"What about me?" he responded.

"Your education. Where did you go to school? What did you study?"

"Oh." Devlin thought about what to tell her and what to keep to himself. He believed in being as honest as possible with clients, but he largely kept his past in the past and shared only details of the present with them.

"I was a troubled teen," he admitted. When she looked doubtful, he said, "No. Really. Always in trouble, in danger of being sent to juvenile hall, the whole nine yards."

"A bad boy," she remarked, her gaze subjecting him to a thorough appraisal. "I guess I can see that."

"Oh, you can, can you?" he teased, but said no more as their coffees and the bill arrived. When she would have grabbed the slip of paper he swiped it away from her. "I'm paying."

"But you're my therapist. I'm supposed to pay for sessions with you, not the other way around."

"Yes," he agreed, "but I invited you, not the other way around, and besides, I said this was both because I had to eat and because I wanted more time with you."

"Okay," she relented, settling back in her seat.

Devlin was glad that she hadn't read the double meaning in his last statement.

"But you still haven't told me about your education," she reminded him.

"Oh, yeah." He tested his coffee's temperature, took a large swallow, and continued with his tale. "So I had a few run-ins with this cop, and he convinced me that I could actually do something with my life. Choosing psychology as a major seemed like the most natural thing in the world. Like your cooking. I had spent my whole life observing what makes people tick."

"And your family?" she asked, after he had paused to take another drink of coffee. "What did they think?"

"I didn't have any," he explained. "Just my best friend. And the cop."

"No family at all?"

"Nope. I was a foster kid. At first it was just me against the world, but when I was nine and he was ten, Mac and I got sent to live at the same hellhole and after that it was always the two of us. We even went through a formal adoption after we grew up. We joke that we're brothers in-law, but we really are. Brothers. Under the law."

Melissa smiled. "What about the cop? Do you still see him?"

"No," Devlin shook his head sadly. "Cancer ate him up. But he got to see me get my bachelor's degree before he died."

"I'm glad," she offered. "But I thought Lexie said you were a doctor?"

"Oh. That." He shrugged as if it was not the big deal that it was for a Southie who grew up in foster care to earn a PhD. "Yeah. That was kind of Mac's doing. After my second try," he indicated his wrists in the leather gauntlets, "Mac told me I should do something constructive with my life. I had some money put away, so I went back to school. It's easy in Boston, with so many great schools, so I enrolled at night for my master's degree, then just kept going."

They had finished their coffees at this point. Devlin paid the bill, left a tip on the table, and suggested that they leave. He might have lingered longer, but a small crowd had gathered in the entryway while the wait staff looked for open seats, so he waited for Melissa to rise and they headed for the exit together.

"Devlin!" a familiar voice hailed him as they approached the door.

"Mac," Devlin said with surprise, automatically stepping in front of Melissa and not even realizing it until he had done it and saw his best friend's eyebrows rise.

Mac was a handsome man. He had prematurely silver hair that women drooled over, a tightly toned body, good manners, and a GQ style of dressing. But that wasn't the only reason he wanted to keep these two apart.

Mac's eyes narrowed. "Introduce me to your friend," he suggested, in a voice that brooked no refusal.

Devlin sighed, stepping to the left so that they could see one another. "Melissa, this is Mac; Mac, this is Melissa," he said.

"Ah," Mac said knowingly. He extended a hand to her, noticed her hesitation in accepting it, but kept it only long enough to say, "It's nice to meet you, Melissa."

"You, too," she nodded. "I've heard a lot about you."

"Oh, really?" Mac questioned, his eyes meeting Devlin's own and promising that he would want the details later.

Less than two hours after they parted, Mac showed up on his doorstep. Or, rather, Mac walked into his condo with the use of the spare keys he possessed and the code he had been given. Not even a knock, just tossing the door back and strolling into the kitchen, a determined look on his face. If Devlin hadn't already been expecting this, he might have prepared to defend the premises against an intruder.

"Talk to me," Mac ordered, grabbing a beer from the refrigerator and taking a seat at the small table before the window where Devlin sat.

"Not much to tell," he responded.

"Wrong answer. Try again."

Devlin eyed his tenacious friend with exasperation, then gave in, "You know who she is. Melissa."

"But I don't know why the two of you are having lunch together in a public place in the middle of the day on a Saturday. Clear enough?" Mac pushed, taking a long draw on his beer but not taking his eyes off Devlin.

"I asked her to lunch."

"Why?"

"We needed to eat?" Devlin suggested sarcastically.

"Don't pull that with me. She's a patient."

"Client."

"Call it whatever you want. You're dodging the question. What are you doing having lunch with her? Doesn't that cross some kind of line for you?"

Devlin sighed, annoyed but knowing that evasion would only make Mac dig in his heels. "I had gone to see her at the immigrant center. She's volunteering there. That's part of her therapy. I did need to eat. Lunch is also part of her therapy."

"Lunch? How so?"

"She is learning to sit across the table from me, make eye contact, share a meal. Those are intimate things and she's afraid of intimacy."

Mac was silent for several minutes. He finished his beer, threw it in the recycle box beside the trash can, sat again.

"Stop seeing her."

"What?" Devlin demanded.

"You heard me. Turn her case over to someone else. Get rid of her as a client."

"Why would I do that?"

"Because you're falling for her," Mac explained.

"And you know this how?" Devlin asked, sarcasm thick in his voice.

"Because I know you, brother. When was the last time you called me?"

Devlin shrugged.

"Right. You start calling less, holding back. I know the signs. You're falling for her and no good can come of it."

"Aren't you the one who said, 'I have a feeling about this?' and 'It could happen'?"

"Forget what I said. I was wrong."

Devlin harrumphed loudly. "You're never wrong."

"I meant the case, brother. I thought her case could help you, because it was like what happened to Masha. You help this woman, you forgive yourself, you finally move on and have a life."

"I am helping her," Devlin shot back defensively.

Mac leaned across the table toward him, grabbing him unexpectedly by the collar of his shirt, his voice earnest as he pressed, "Get rid of her, Dev. You're going down the same road you traveled before. I can see it. Get out before you get in any deeper."

Devlin threw off Mac's hand, rising from his seat and pacing to the living room doorway and back. "Bullshit," he finally said. "There is no similarity between that time and now."

Mac knew when Devlin was approachable and when the mule in him came out. Right now it was a wonder there wasn't braying in the room, because Devlin was digging in and refusing to listen.

"I love you, brother," Mac said quietly. "You know I only want what's best for you." He turned and went to the door, taking the knob in his hand and stepping into the doorway before turning back to say, "I'm just afraid that this time when you fall, you might crash so hard and so fast that I won't be able to catch you."

Chapter 15
The Raid

He had only had six more weeks with Masha before the raid came. During that time he worked relentlessly to give her knowledge. She still wore the ankle bracelet, he still didn't let her out of his sight, and at night he tied her to the bed they shared to prevent an escape attempt, but he did everything he could to equip her with tools for survival. He made her memorize Mac's cell phone number in case anything happened to him and taught her to say, "I am calling for Ryan MacGilvary. My name is Masha Wozny. I need your help."

They worked on practical knowledge as well as safety. On the weekends they would go shopping and he would make her recite the names of items in the grocery store and department store from pictures in flyers that he saved to go over with her. At night they played Scrabble and practiced numbers, first with a deck of cards, then with common items like toothpicks and cotton balls, and finally they worked on money, making change, and price ranges that were acceptable. In the morning he played his guitar for her and taught her every patriotic and traditional American song he knew.

At her request he bought her a cookbook. She burned a few things, including coffee, and a couple of times she misread the fractions on recipes so that some foods rose that weren't supposed to while others fell flat, but she seemed to really like cooking so he ate most of her attempts without comment. He even enjoyed the Ukrainian foods she made.

He grew to love her with each passing day. She was smart, feisty, and funny despite her circumstances. He was amazed at how intelligent she was and how a girl like that could have ended up in the situation she was in, but he understood con artists. If they weren't convincing and believable, it wouldn't be called a con.

Mac had tried to tell him then that it wasn't love. Although they only communicated by telephone, and only on the weekends, Devlin had confided in his foster brother that he was in love with the Ukrainian girl. Mac told him to use his psychology background and think again about his feelings. That he couldn't be in love with her because she wasn't free to love him. He was the captor; she was the captive. He felt guilt over his behavior and she felt dependence on him. That wasn't love. Devlin told his best friend to shove his opinions up his ass and stopped calling him except to check in, ending those calls before they could say anything beyond a greeting.

He knew what he felt for Masha, and it was more than just a sense of responsibility. He liked her. He was attracted to her. After that trip to D.C. their relationship changed. They kissed. They held hands. When they began soft petting in that last month, it was not a protective big brother or a ruthless kidnapper involved with her. It was a man, loving a woman, and trying to express his emotions through physical means. He knew what Mac would say; she was shackled to him and had no choice. But she did more than just not turn away from him. She turned toward him.

It was at the end of that month when they returned to the camp on a Sunday night with a bag full of fish, a small tank, and everything they needed to keep the fish alive in it. Earlier that day he had taken her to the New England Aquarium. Her enthusiasm for the trip made some of the kids there look bored by comparison. She moved from glass to glass, prattling away in a mixture of English and Ukrainian, pointing to exhibits and smiling, throwing out her hands in amazement. She explained that she had never seen the ocean before that day, that the closest she had come to it was looking out the window of the plane on her flight to America, and that she had always wanted to see it. So they toured the aquarium, walked up and down the wharves, dined at a restaurant with a harbor view, and when she asked if they could have a fish tank of their own, he didn't even consider saying no.

Neither one of them knew anything about keeping fish, of course. They had to rely on the sales clerk at the pet store to help them pick species that wouldn't eat one another. Then there was the filter, the stones, the little fake trees and hideaway structures. Devlin started to think that a puppy would be less work even if it did pee all over the cabin, but Masha was elated and he was determined to make her happy. So when she suggested that they sleep on the floor to keep watch over the shiny finned creatures on their first night, he agreed to that as well. But when her affection turned more eager than usual, he gently put a stop to it by turning her away from him and tucking her backside up against his body, distracting her by pointing at the fish. He didn't want their first time to be motivated by gratitude. He didn't want their first time to be on hard wood.

The following night was another story. He had finished work at the lodge before joining her for a late supper of borscht and pampushkas with the usual sour cream on the side. They alternated between Ukrainian food and American food, but no matter what she made it was always good. She had a real talent for cooking. Devlin showed his appreciation by eating every last bite of the beef and beet soup. When he would have licked his fingers clean of the garlic left from holding the pampushkas, Masha stilled his hand. He looked at her, puzzled. She loved to watch him lick his fingers. She saw it as the ultimate compliment for her cooking.

To say he was surprised when she brought the tip of one digit to her own mouth and curled her tongue around it would have been an understatement. His heart rate doubled. His temperature spiked. His cock leaped. Every part of his body was alert and ready, but he sat exactly where he was and let her take the lead.

When she pulled his finger into her mouth and suckled it, he dug his heels into the floor, the rest of his body going rigid. She smiled at him with her wide hazel eyes and did the same thing to the next finger, and the next. By the time she moved on to his other hand his breathing was loud in the room, so ragged it hurt his chest.

"You want me now," she whispered, the words hesitant but the inflection flat. Devlin knew her well enough to recognize that she was asking him a question rather than making a statement.

"God, yes," he replied, the admission painfully torn from him. He had never wanted anyone like this before. Would never want anyone like this again.

"Come?" she said, rising and extending her hand to him. Again the inflection was off, because this time she was definitely not asking a question. She was issuing an order and Devlin was only too happy to let her.

He put his hand in her own and rose from the chair, walking over to the bed and sitting down on the comforter beside her. They had slept in this bed night after night, wrapped around one another. They had both seen and been seen in various states of dress and undress, but this was different. Tonight when she took hold of the hem of her shirt and lifted it up over her torso it was not to replace it with something for sleeping in. When her fingers slipped the clasp of her bra free and peeled the edges back to reveal her small, firm breasts it was not to step into the shower and bathe.

Bravado could only carry her so far, though. After dropping the shirt and bra to the floor where they joined the shoes she had slipped from her feet, she looked up at him with wide eyes full of longing and uncertainty. She didn't know what to do next. Their petting had been mostly in the dark and at the adolescent level. What she wanted now was beyond her experience.

Devlin moved slowly. Giving her time to change her mind, he removed his own shirt. Stood and shucked his jeans, kicked off his shoes and rolled the stockings from his feet. When he resumed his seat on the bed, the only thing left on his body was a pair of boxer shorts that did little to hide his arousal.

Masha's eyes widened at the tenting of the cotton fabric that covered him. Her jaw went a little slack, but she looked intrigued. When she extended the tip of one finger to touch him through the material, his cock leapt in response and she jumped, mouth forming an "O" of surprise.

Devlin smiled at her reaction. He admired her courage. He enjoyed the way her breasts had jiggled when she moved. Wanting to show her a little of what he felt, he extended his own hands, curled the index fingers on each around her small pink nipples and flicked them softly back and forth, pebbling the flesh. She shivered and broke out in goose bumps. Her hands went slack in her lap, palms open, her eyes dazed.

Smiling again at both her response and her trusting posture,

Devlin wrapped the palm of one hand around her breast while continuing to gently toy with the nipple on the other. Never taking his eyes from her face, he leaned forward and, lifting that breast with his palm, he kissed it.

Masha shuddered. Her eyes lost their glazed look, but now they were fever bright. Devlin saluted that breast again, using his tongue this time and, when she moaned softly, repeated the action. Then he slowly laid her back against the comforter, followed her down, and settled beside her where he could freely pleasure that same breast as much as he wanted to.

She placed her hands uncertainly on his bare shoulders. Dug her fingers unconsciously into his skin when he took the nipple lightly between his teeth and tugged at it. Lost all semblance of control when he then blew softly on the wet flesh. Her hands fell limply at her sides and her torso rose up to meet him. He did it again and watched with pleasure as her head rolled from side to side.

Devlin took the whole nipple with his mouth then. He suckled on it like a babe would suckle at his mother's breast, his eyes closed, but his senses open. She had to be with him on this. He couldn't go too fast or play too rough. There could be no question of force, no chance of losing her to memories of her first sexual experience.

Masha convulsed beneath him. Slid her fingers across the short bristles of his hair and held him to her. Rubbed her pelvis against the thigh that rested on top of it, her legs scissoring restlessly against his own.

He worshipped her body. Went from breast to breast until she was panting and shaking from the sensations. He unsnapped her jeans and celebrated inside when she lifted her hips to help him with their removal at the same time that she clasped his head to her breast.

Devlin made wide circles against her naked waist, her hip, and her thigh with his free hand. Each time he went a little lower. Came a little closer to that part of her that should only be offered as a gift.

Masha shivered when his fingers neared the top of her inner thigh. Scraped her fingernails down his back and made a yearning sound deep in her throat.

He touched her then. Not the way he would touch a woman

with experience, but lightly, exploring her reaction.

She dug her heels into the comforter and rocked against his fingers. Above his head he could hear her panting softly, could see from the corner of his eyes that she was tossing her head back and forth on the pillow.

He abandoned her breasts, then slid up against her body and took her mouth with his own. She grabbed onto him like he was a life raft. Tangled her tongue with his own, held fast to his head and shoulders, lifted her hips to him and made soft, incoherent sounds of need.

Devlin slid a finger inside her body and groaned at the warm welcome there. Masha almost came off the bed. She might be inexperienced, but she knew what she liked, and when that finger started moving and he added pressure with his thumb to the clitoris above it, she tore her mouth away from his own and buried her face in his neck.

"Bite me," he suggested, knowing that she was looking for a way to handle the sensations buffeting her body and that putting her teeth to his shoulder would give her that control, but of course she didn't. She was innocent. Her English was not sophisticated enough to understand the suggestion in this context. And she was fast losing her mind to his lovemaking.

Devlin had to admit that he was flattered. Of course he had been with other women, had gone through a stage in college where he needed to prove that he was attractive to women and not men, had to reclaim and define his own sexuality. That meant a lot of time in the bedroom. But he had never pleased a woman like he was pleasing Masha now. Had never even wanted to.

"I love you," he admitted, adding a second finger to the first and watching as her eyes squeezed tightly closed and her teeth clamped down on her lower lip in reaction. Devlin kissed the tendon that stood out on the side of her neck. Sipped his way up to her ear and pulled the lobe between his teeth. Her eyes flew open wide and a shiver raced over her skin. "I love you," he repeated before laving the soft cartilage with his tongue.

Masha bucked against him in reaction. Her eyes sought his, desperate with need, unaware of what was happening to her. "Please help me, Mick," she pleaded.

"My Masha," he groaned, sliding his fingers from her body and levering himself up on his elbows so he could take off his boxer shorts. He kissed her mouth, her shoulder, her nipple while using one hand to ready himself and position her thighs so that he wouldn't hurt her. Then he slid home.

She still didn't know what to do with her legs so he lifted them, showing her how to hold on with her ankles. She smiled and kissed him for that. Then he started to move inside her and her hazel eyes glazed over again.

"Talk to me," he whispered at her ear, flattered that she was losing herself to their lovemaking but wanting her with him all the way.

"No talking," she gasped. She pushed her heels into his thighs for leverage and raised her hips against him. "Talk later. Do this now!"

The last was almost a command and Devlin rejoiced in it.

"Whatever the lady wants."

He grasped her thighs and pulled them higher against his sides. Rocked his pelvis against hers and added a finger to the friction between them there. Plumped a breast with his other hand, bringing it to his mouth for his attention. As soon as he took the nipple onto his tongue, she started to shake. Her hips rose and fell spasmodically. Perspiration glistened against her skin, trickling into her hair and making strands of the light brown mane cling to her forehead, her cheeks, her neck.

She shattered. That was the only way to describe what happened when, one moment she was drawn taut as a bow and in the next she fell to pieces, losing control of her limbs and shaking apart. That was when he found his own release. Tensed, bucked, and finally followed her down onto the bed where they both lay spent, muscles lax, breathing ragged.

Masha moved first. Sliding a hand over his shorn head she nudged his chin until he turned to look at her, his cheek resting on her bare shoulder.

"You love me," she said, more a question than statement.

She probably didn't believe it, probably thought that he said it only in the throes of passion. "I love you," Devlin told her simply.

Hazel eyes grew solemn, watered up a little.

Devlin kissed her shoulder, rolled away and pulled her against his side, tucking her head beneath his chin. He used his other hand to yank the comforter out from beneath them and cover their fast cooling bodies.

"I love you, my Masha," he said again. "I will always love you." He gave her a squeeze before reaching up to turn off the light switch above the headboard.

"I would know you anywhere," he whispered, kissing her temple. "I would find you anywhere. Even in the dark I would know it was you."

He didn't think she heard him. Thought she was probably asleep already. But just as he was about to slip into his own dark oblivion he heard her say, "I love you too, Mick."

Devlin slept soundly, planning to talk with her later about their feelings and their future, but the raid came the day after their one and only night of lovemaking.

They hadn't warned him of the timing, only that they were getting close. So when he woke in the early morning hours to a gun in his face, his first thought was that Kraus had found him out. Blinking, he looked up and saw not the Czech, but one of his supervisors staring back at him.

"It's time," Martin said, "Now put on a show."

Devlin had to pretend to be a criminal. He fought with the other man, tried to wrest the gun from his hand, yelled for Masha to run! Got in a couple of punches just for good measure before two of them wrestled him to the floor, a knee in his back to hold him there. He swore and snarled at them when they tripped in their pursuit of Masha and the fish tank went over, crashing into pieces; looked on with real heartache when she turned back, crying out in dismay at the sight of her new pets floundering on the wood. Devlin saw her try to scoop them up and save them, only to be grabbed by the arms herself and escorted out the door.

He had no choice but to let them handcuff him and put him into a police car to be driven away. Could do nothing but watch as they put Masha in another car, without the cuffs but still seated behind a grilled divider, hazel eyes wide with terror and seeking him out across the distance that separated them. Kraus was put in a third car, trying his slimy charm on the officers and insisting that there was a mistake; he was just a caretaker at the camp and hadn't broken any laws.

They let him speak to her in one of the interrogation rooms, a gray cell of a room with no window unless the two-way mirror could be counted as one. Masha sat in the corner, huddled away from everyone, shaking like a leaf until he walked in. Then he opened his arms and she ran into them, crying, afraid. A Russian translator was brought in and using Masha's second language and one that Devlin didn't know at all, he was able to convey the situation to her. That he had been working undercover as a cop. That he was sorry for all that had happened to her. That she would be safe now but in order to keep her safe they would have to be separated. He also told her that he loved her, something the translator refused to repeat, but for that Devlin didn't need the woman anyway. He had learned enough at the immigrant center during his time as a volunteer to know how to express the feelings, so he pointed to his chest, placed his hand over his heart, and pointed to the traumatized girl in his arms while saying the words, "I. Love. You."

Following that declaration, he was ushered out of Masha's interrogation room and sent for debriefing, something that lasted for days. By the time his superiors had finished with him, Masha was gone, secured at the Connecticut facility, and he was told to forget they had ever met. As if he could.

Chapter 16
Sweet Torture

Tuesday was a perfect spring day. People all over Boston came out of hibernation, threw off their winter coats, left their umbrellas at home, and reveled in the sunshine that bathed the harbors, rivers, and monuments of the city. It was the worst possible day to spend in court.

When they adjourned for a long lunch, he grabbed some food at Faneuil Hall and walked over Beacon Hill to the Common to eat. He sat at the top, near the bronze frieze of the 54th Massachusetts marching off to fight in the Civil War. Below him children ran around in circles, couples lounged on towels or blankets, and groups of people in work clothing sat on the grass, chatting idly beneath the long dormant sunshine. Behind him a National Park Ranger met a group of high school students to give them a tour of the African American Heritage Trail, which began at the frieze.

Devlin took it all in and wished that he was not sitting here alone. He wanted to share this beautiful day and these sights and sounds. The problem was he didn't know who he wanted to share it with. Was it Masha? Or was it Melissa? He thought about Mac's warning for a moment but dismissed it just as quickly. He was not lost again. Not hovering on the brink of darkness. He just had some soul searching to do.

Back in court he suffered through several cases before being given sixty seconds to provide his expert opinion on behalf of the Commonwealth. The judge made a decision that was in line with that opinion, rapped her gavel, and Devlin was free to leave.

Outside once more, he grabbed the T and rode it to the hospital where Melissa worked, but once he stood in front of the main entrance, he didn't know what to do. Didn't understand the impulse that had made him get off at this stop. Was it just to see where she spent her days? He wouldn't do that with his other clients. Remembering the way he had felt when the surrogate touched her, he thought again about Mac's warning. Was he right? As much as Devlin hated to admit it, Mac was rarely wrong. The fact that Devlin was standing here when he hadn't been in the neighborhood, wasn't just passing by, and had no reason to make contact in between sessions, shook him.

This was stalker behavior. There was nothing professional about it. If Melissa came outside and saw him standing there, what would she think? She had already been victim to one sexual predator. Here he was acting no better than that other man. He was crossing a line, one that separated the light from the dark, and the realization scared him. Breaking out into a cold sweat, he hurried to get on the T again and rode it back to the courthouse where he got his Scout from the parking garage attendant and headed home. Where he would be safe from himself.

He met Mac for dinner on Thursday. Not at a restaurant this time, but at Mac's posh living space in the Back Bay. A waterway that was filled in and made into high-end houses, it represented wealth. Success. Stability. All of the things that Mac had worked his life to accomplish and that Devlin could take or leave.

"Hey, brother," Mac greeted him at the door in stocking feet, thumping him on the back with one hand, a spatula in the other. "Figured we should have hamburgers on a day like this."

"Sounds good to me," Devlin remarked. "It's like June out there."

"Yeah. But just wait a minute—"

"—and it'll change," they finished together.

Mac went back to the stove and Devlin helped himself to a glass of water from a bottle in the fridge. He sipped it as he wandered over to the wall-sized fish tank separating the living area from the entry. "See you got a couple of new ones," he noted.

"Yeah. Lexie and Ernest gave them to me as thanks for introducing them."

Devlin grunted noncommittally.

"I told them the thanks should go to you, but..."

"But I don't keep fish and she would probably rather see me gutted like one."

Mac shook his head, sliding the burgers off the stove's griddle and onto waiting buns. "Come on. Let's eat."

They had potato salad and chips with the burgers. When they finished, Mac grabbed a couple of beers from the fridge and they moved into the living room to sit and watch ESPN together. Tonight the talk was all about the Celtics, how the playoffs were expected to go, and what their chances were for a good pick in the NBA draft come June. They listened for a few minutes before Mac switched the channel.

"So what's new with you?" Devlin asked, idly watching some report on high school students and standardized test scores.

"I've got my eyes on a project," Mac shared.

"Oh? Anything you want to tell me about?"

"Not yet. I just have to wait for some other things to fall into place before I can make my move, then I'll tell you all about it."

"Big profit involved?" Devlin questioned.

"No. This one's not about the money."

"Now I am intrigued."

They were quiet for a few minutes while the reporter droned on about national politics.

"I won't take back what I said," Mac finally spoke, bringing their last exchange out into the open.

"I know," Devlin nodded.

"I meant all of it."

"I know."

"But I'll be there if you need me, Dev. Always."

"I know that too, brother," Devlin replied.

Friday was a mild form of torture for Devlin. He had an intake evaluation in the morning that was a complete waste of his time. It was obvious that the husband was only there under duress, did not believe that he and his wife needed any help, and was completely closed to the idea that a psychologist could change their relationship. It was 'all in her head', he said several times until finally Devlin stopped the evaluation. He told them bluntly that their problem was bigger than the bedroom and that it would never improve until the husband recognized that he was the main source of that problem. So the husband told him where he could stick his degrees and walked out.

The afternoon was filled with regulars, but he had a hard time concentrating on their needs. He found himself looking at the clock surreptitiously, something he never did when clients were before him, so when the last appointment of the day called to cancel with a lame excuse, he was grateful.

Now he just had three and a half hours to kill. He drove to the club, found a sparring partner in the dungeon and boxed until he thought he might pass out if he went another round. That fatigue lasted only until he finished showering. Then he was back to being almost dangerously excited. Luckily he had made a list of things he needed for the night so he had something constructive to do with part of the remaining time.

Devlin went first to his rental storage unit and retrieved the smooth wooden bench he kept there. It looked a little like a sawhorse but sat lower to the ground and had double grooves on each side. From there he went to a Yankee Candle distributor and searched until he found just the right product. It was a tall candle in a jar with the mildest of spruce scents and a domed frosted top made to let the light shine out while a hole in the top let the air in to keep the flame alive. Finally he went back to the office where he set up the treatment room, called the surrogate to fill him in on the night's plans, then sat to wait for Melissa.

She arrived clad in a simple cotton dress with a U-shaped neckline, long loose sleeves, and a slightly flared skirt. She had pumps on her feet and a silver circlet dangled from a chain around her neck. Her blond hair was pulled back into a tight little bun that he wanted to take down.

Keep it professional, he reminded himself, asking, "Did you come straight from work?"

"Yes. We had a dinner meeting with some insurance reps, and it just ended," she explained.

"Ah," he nodded. "Do you have something more comfortable to wear?"

"Yes, sir." She indicated a plastic bag in her hand.

"Well, I have a couple of things to do before we get started, so I'd like you to go into the bathroom to change, then I'll call you when everything is ready."

"Okay," she said, uncertainty showing in her eyes as she moved slowly to do as he told her.

"Trust me," Devlin smiled, anticipation thrumming through his veins.

In the treatment room he had put the candle where the therapy light usually sat and moved the straight-backed chair off to the side to be replaced with the bench. Because he didn't want Melissa to panic at the sight of these changes, he turned off the main light and used the glow from an illuminated keychain to find the bathroom door.

"You can come out now," he told her, stepping out of the way for her to do just that.

She emerged dressed in a long worn t-shirt over soft cotton shorts and slipper socks on her feet.

"No lights?" she asked, a tremor in her voice indicating that she was still not completely comfortable with the dark.

"There will be," he assured her, taking her hand and leading her over to the bench.

She started groping for the back of the chair, but he stilled her movements, guiding her instead to sit on the smooth wooden surface then turn until she was straddling the piece of furniture. He squeezed her shoulder, said, "I'll be right back," and crossed the room to set up the candle.

"No light?" she asked again when he returned.

"I don't think you need the therapy light any more. Just look into the flame," he instructed, sliding onto the bench behind her.

"Watch the way it flickers." He leaned down and ran the padded restraint along the back of her calf, all the way to her ankle where he fastened it then clicked the other half around the middle leg of the bench. "Deep breaths," he reminded her as his hand made a return journey.

Devlin had a lot more access to her body with the bench than he had with the chair. The grooves on either side allowed her legs to splay out comfortably so that only her buttocks rested on the surface. He planned to take advantage of that.

"How are you doing, Melissa?" he questioned, slipping the key into her right hand.

"Okay, I guess," she answered.

"Good. Just keep looking at the candle. It will do the same thing the light did, just in slow motion. Now take a deep breath."

She did.

He slipped off the bench and moved back so the surrogate could replace him.

"Another deep breath," Devlin told her, watching as the other man ran his hands up her arms and beneath the loose sleeves of her t-shirt to find her shoulders beneath.

"Again."

The surrogate massaged her shoulders briefly before pulling the collar of her shirt aside so that he could plant a kiss on the right side of her neck.

"Good girl," Devlin murmured while the other man blew softly against her skin, and she shuddered in response.

With his mouth, the surrogate continued to sip at her neck, her shoulder, and her ear. His hands, in the meantime, made a slow slide back down her arms until he placed her hands on her upper thighs and smoothed over them to touch the soft flesh beneath. Melissa shivered deliciously, a jagged breath escaping her.

Devlin braced himself against the wall, needing to watch and at the same time hating to watch as the other man pulled her earlobe between his teeth, laved it with his tongue, and was rewarded when she rolled her head back against his shoulder and pushed her hips forward.

"Melissa, when was the last time you had an orgasm?" Devlin

whispered.

She jerked at the question, but the other man's teeth held her ear and his hands held her knees, so she didn't go far.

"Tell me," Devlin persisted.

"But you know there hasn't been anyone. Not since him."

"John. Say his name for me."

"Not since John," she rushed out breathlessly as the surrogate's hands found their way up the inside of her thighs beneath the loose shorts she wore and came dangerously close to the line of her panties.

Devlin's control almost broke at the sight.

He forced himself to continue. "But that's not what I asked you, Melissa. I asked when you last had an orgasm."

"I'm not sure," she replied.

"Take a guess," Devlin insisted, watching as the surrogate's hands circled the insides of her upper thighs and he blew lightly against her ear.

"I don't know," she said.

"A year? A month? A week?"

"No, I mean I'm not sure if I've had an orgasm before," she elaborated.

Devlin went still at her reply and just hoped the surrogate didn't do the same. Since that could disrupt their rhythm and her progress toward relaxation, he forced himself to continue on as if he was unsurprised. He also needed to make sure that he understood her answer.

"But you have masturbated?"

She grew still now. Devlin couldn't allow that.

The surrogate, understanding, renewed his assault on her neck and shoulder, drew larger circles on her inner thighs.

"I'm waiting," Devlin reminded her patiently.

"Not really," she admitted. "I've touched myself." Her voice dropped to a barely audible level. "But I didn't really know what I was doing, and it didn't seem to help any. I tried thinking of him."

"John."

"Yes, John. I tried thinking of him, but nothing really happened. I got excited for a few minutes, but that was all. It didn't really seem to work for me."

The surrogate nuzzled the skin behind her ear, sending tremors down her spine.

"Well I'm going to change that," Devlin promised, wishing he was on the bench behind her instead of the other man. "Tonight you'll have your first orgasm."

Melissa tensed at his pronouncement, but the surrogate kept his touch light until she had relaxed back into a steady breathing pattern and her spine lost its stiffness. Then he moved along the bench so that his hips were cradling her own and her shoulders rested against his chest.

"The light, Melissa," Devlin reminded her, adding, "Just keep looking into the light and you'll have nothing to worry about."

The other man ran his hands up to the tops of her thighs beneath the loose shorts. Let his thumbs rake out across her panty lines. Her breathing hitched, became ragged. Devlin's breathing mirrored her own, though he was careful to keep her from hearing it.

"The key is in your hand. You can stop this whenever you want," he reminded her, part of him wishing that she would.

She made an inarticulate sound that might have had something to do with what he was saying but was more likely because at that moment the surrogate slipped one hand beneath her t-shirt to rest against her belly just below the navel. He didn't move it, just held it there, anchoring her against him.

When she had accepted that touch, his other hand followed the first but kept going. Across her flat stomach and up to her small naked breasts, cupping the weight of one in his palm. His tongue snaked out and curled around her ear, his breath rushing over her, sending visible chills down her body even as she warmed to his touch.

Devlin moved closer. Because he couldn't help himself.

"Have you touched yourself there?" Devlin asked as the surrogate flicked his thumb across her peaked nipple.

She shrank away from the other man's hand but had nowhere to go.

"Have you?" Devlin repeated, and the action was repeated as well. "Yes," she admitted softly.

"And did you like it?"

"It made me feel funny," she confessed.

Devlin already knew that feeling funny to Melissa meant that she was turned on. So he nodded to the other man who then dedicated himself to that nipple as though it was his job. Which it was, but Devlin wished he wasn't quite so good at it. He wanted to be the one to bring her pleasure.

The surrogate slipped Melissa's hands from the sleeves of her shirt and rolled it up so that it rested on her shoulders, baring her upper body to his touch and to Devlin's view.

"No," she objected, pulling the material down to cover herself.

"Okay," Devlin said reassuringly, using the power of his voice to calm her and calling himself all sorts of vile names because he had enjoyed that brief glimpse of her nipples, puckering against the air.

The surrogate rubbed his thumb over the tip of her nipple again and again, until she returned to the state she had been in before he pulled up her shirt. With his thumb and forefinger he grasped that same tip, pulled on it lightly, then rolled it in his grasp.

Melissa's breath exhaled in a rush. She alternately shrank away from his ministrations and sought them, her hips beginning to undulate against him in a rhythm as old as time while her back arched and bowed, arched and bowed. Devlin wondered if the man's cock was hard. If so, she didn't seem to notice. His own certainly was.

The surrogate moved his other hand. Sliding the fingers beneath the top of her panties, he brushed against the soft delta there. His caress was slow while his other hand grew bolder. The double stimulation had her increasing her movements. She was reaching for something but didn't know what it was. Devlin did.

Sliding the soles of his feet up the front of her ankles, the other man caressed the inside of them with his toes. His mouth dropped a line of kisses from her shoulder to her ear and back again. His left hand played with the nipple on that same side, his right hand made ever-widening circles on the lowest part of her belly, and she moved in harmony with his actions.

The surrogate angled her across his lap so that he could reach the right nipple with his mouth while the left remained firmly in his grasp. As soon as he nuzzled the t-shirt out of his way and latched onto the tender tip, Melissa let go of a keening cry.

"Oh, yeah," Devlin encouraged, watching as the other man suckled on her nipple, then laved it with his tongue. He continued to pull on and pet its mate.

She was shaking now. Her breathing was choppy and shallow. Devlin actually bent over and braced his hands against his knees, wondering if he had ever felt so tortured in his life.

The surrogate slid his feet up the length of her shins and across her calves until they were wrapped around her legs, spreading them further apart and holding them in place with the weight of his thighs against her own. She bucked once in reaction.

"Mmm-hmmm," Devlin murmured encouragingly, amazed that he could make any sense at all.

Melissa could not stay still any longer. At first her hands had flopped loosely at her sides, lost for purpose, but now she reached up to hold the surrogate's head against her breast with one hand while the other pushed his hand against the opposite nipple.

"Help him there," Devlin croaked.

"Hmm?" she questioned.

Clearing his throat, Devlin clarified, "Play with your nipple." The surrogate breathed against the one he was ministering to. "Pull it. Roll it. Show him what you like."

Hesitantly at first, then gaining in confidence, she did as he told her to. The surrogate shaped and molded the breast with his hand and together they tortured the tip until her breathing was loud in the room.

Devlin found that he was standing just a few feet away from them and didn't know when he had moved.

The other man abandoned his gentle foreplay at her belly and slid his hand lower. Imagining where it was going, picturing it sliding through the soft folds of her skin, seeking the small piece of flesh nestled at the top of them, had Devlin fighting with the need to move closer. In his mind he could picture the surrogate tugging at that flesh while his other hand was at her breast. He knew the man had his mouth at her breast already.

Devlin broke out in a cold sweat.

Chapter 17

Fire in the Veins

"Oh my God," Melissa breathed, rocking back and forth against the man behind her.

"Good?" Devlin murmured, but it came out as more of a gasp for air.

"So good," she moaned, lost to the sensations of professional lovemaking. "So good," she repeated.

The surrogate started to move against her. With his feet trapping her legs and his hips surrounding her own, his hands on the front of her, he played her body like an orchestra. Increasing the tempo, bringing out more volume, changing the pitch, until a little climax hit and the note was held for an extended period of time, then broke and dropped back down again.

Melissa slumped against the other man. So naïve. She probably thought that they were through.

At a nod from Devlin, the surrogate brought his mouth back up to her neck and ear, licking and sucking, kissing and biting. His left hand pushed her breasts together and he shared his thumb with both nipples, taking turns rolling it across each one. His right hand, having stilled while she caught her breath, started moving again at her clitoris.

"But?" she asked, puzzled, her hips already undulating against the erection at her back.

"That was just the prelude," Devlin promised.

He could see her swallow.

"Put your hand where his hand is," Devlin told her, clarifying, "down there."

Hesitantly she followed his directions.

The surrogate used his hand to guide her index finger into place against the swollen little nerve center. "That's right. Now rub it back and forth, in circles," Devlin said.

She did as he instructed, panting almost immediately, her elbow sawing against her side as she fought to reach that same place she had been just minutes before.

Devlin could almost feel her disappointment when she came to the edge, again and again, but could never go over into the sweet abyss.

"Let him help," Devlin whispered, and when she nodded, the other man slid his middle finger up inside her body.

She wailed. Devlin wanted to howl.

He liked her honest reactions. She might be inexperienced, but that meant that she didn't pretend either.

The surrogate started to move his finger in time with her own strokes against her clit and the movements of his other hand against her breast. He added his feet to the action, stroking up and down against the inside of her calves. His mouth latched onto her breast and suckled.

"Oh my, oh my," she panted, her movements almost out of control as she rode the wooden bench, bucked against his lap, and threw her head back against his shoulder.

"Mr. O'Malley!" she called helplessly, straining for relief, release.

Devlin actually took a step forward, caught himself just in time, turned away and raked his fingers through his thick hair but found himself turning back, unable to look away even though it was causing him pain.

The surrogate added another finger to the first. Used his thumb to add pressure to the finger at her clit. Sucked her nipple between his teeth and pinched the other one.

Melissa started shaking as the orgasm rolled over her like a tidal wave. Tremors wracked her body, then she was riding the other man's hand as fast as she could, racing for the finish line. Even when it hit her and she seized up in his arms, muscles clenched against the sweet agony of her release, he didn't stop. His tongue at one breast, hand at the other, feet on her bare legs and fingers inside and out-side of her body, he tormented every last drop of ecstasy from her.

Only when she collapsed against him and even the internal convulsions had stopped did the surrogate gradually ease back. He graced her nipple with a kiss before easing his head away from it and resting his chin against her shoulder. The other hand gentled its hold on her breast, brushing softly against it, rearranging her t-shirt until it covered her, then smoothing it down against her body, pulling her close against him. His feet slid unhurriedly back down to her ankles then onto the floor outside where her own feet rested, using his thighs to nudge hers closer together. Then he removed one finger from inside her, feathered his thumb against the outside of her swollen nether lips a few times, then removed the other finger, using that hand to right her panties then cup her in a hold that was meant to reassure.

"Melissa," Devlin said softly.

She grunted a little bit in response.

"I'm going to ask you to sit up now."

The surrogate used his torso as a brace, sitting up straight so that she had no choice but to do the same, then brought his left hand around from the front of her shirt to her shoulder, holding her steady.

"Okay so far?" Devlin asked.

"Mmm-hmm."

Slowly the man at her back slid his other hand away from the core of her, across her thigh and outer hip until it, too, was placed at her shoulder.

"Do you know where the key is?" Devlin questioned.

She looked to her hand, then shook her head.

"That's okay."

Devlin motioned the surrogate away and when the other man had left the room he came to stand beside Melissa at the bench. She was completely boneless. He helped her to recline until she was lying back against the bench. Then he moved to the center leg and lifted it so that the restraint fell away from the furniture but remained secure around her ankle. When she didn't move, he scooped her spine up off the wooden surface and guided her over to the sofa bed.

"The key?" she asked drowsily.

"The key is on the floor someplace," he told her as he laid her gently down on the cushions. "I don't think we need to use it any longer."

"Hmm," she purred. There was no other word for the satisfied sound that came out of her.

Devlin kissed her forehead, ran his hand against her cheek in a brief caress, and stepped away from her. If he didn't move now, he was going to do something he might regret later. So he snuffed the candle, turned on the bathroom light, and hoisting the bench into his grasp, told her to go ahead and get dressed while he ran the item out to his vehicle. There he spent several minutes getting himself under control and giving her the time she needed to do the same.

He stayed away from the center on Saturday. His emotions were all over the place and if he couldn't get a handle on them, he was pretty sure that Melissa was experiencing the same thing so he decided that time and space were called for.

The weekend was beautiful as only springtime in Boston can be. Over in Cambridge the crew teams were practicing on the Charles River. Runners were out in force. Trees unfurled their leaves and flowers bloomed. On Pleasure Bay a fundraising walk for the Humane Society was being held. People from all around brought their dogs to meet at Castle Island. The concession stand served string cheese and hot dogs while a smart vendor offered water in disposable cardboard bowls. Devlin strolled among them, enjoying the sun on his face and the carefree spirit that filled the assembled group. He dropped a donation into the organizer's hand, explaining that he didn't have a dog, but that it looked like they had enough sponsored walkers to make the day a success.

When he had crossed the bridge to the island and back a couple of times, he decided to go for a drive. He didn't have any particular destination in mind, which was okay in his hometown because the roads meandered all over the place in a pattern that was no pattern to those unfamiliar with them. Eventually he found himself on

Route 3 headed south. He had the windows down in the Scout, letting the warm breeze run through the vehicle from both sides. When it was time to decide between east and west, he chose east. That took him down to the Cape.

In their pre-teen years Devlin and Mac had been sent to the 4-H camp in Mashpee. Because they were less than a full year apart, in the summers they were the same age so they got to attend the same sessions. Devlin still had great memories of that time away. He wasn't sure if it was the camp itself or just knowing that they were safe from the pedophile who housed them, but the memories were good ones nonetheless.

It was a short trip from the highway in Sandwich to Camp Farley on the west side of Mashpee Pond. No one was around at this time of year. Houses along the Cape were preparing for summer, opening shutters and rooting through storage sheds for gardening equipment, but the camp would remain dormant until schools let out. Then the counselors would arrive to train for the summer and when that was done a combination of day and overnight programs would start.

Mac probably got his love of exercise in this place, Devlin thought as he parked the Scout and made his way through the woods to the main lodge. Or it might have been later, when he was incarcerated at Deer Island for beating their foster father to a pulp for hurting Devlin one too many times.

Devlin had come away from the camp with something else. It was here that he discovered his love of watching people. Happy people. Lonely people. People with a genuine desire to make an experience good for others. People who couldn't wait for the weekend to come and with it freedom. He began to wonder what events in the lives of others were responsible for making them who they were and why two people could react differently to the same experience.

He could mark those times and people in his life that had changed the path he would travel. Being taken away from his junkie mother. Meeting Mac when they were both put in the same home. Being raped by his foster father. Coming here to camp. Running up against Sergeant Webster. Volunteering at the immigrant center. Going to police academy and accepting the undercover assignment.

Masha. Melissa.

Devlin wandered around the camp for a little while, reflecting on his life and its various twists and turns. Then the sun began to slide across the continent, leaving shadows over the eastern seaboard, and he headed back to his Scout. By the time he pulled up in front of his condo it was dusk. He congratulated himself for staying away from Melissa, was proud of himself for not spending the whole day thinking about her, and he was saddened to realize that he did not feel unfaithful to Masha for the times when he had. ***

Devlin gave a guest lecture at UMass Lowell on Tuesday morning about the stages of sexual development in individuals and what can happen to adolescents when a stage is disrupted. Something he knew a lot about, given his own youth, not to mention his experience with Masha. But for a change he did not dwell on that. Instead, he traveled down to the city and his office with nothing but anticipation pumping through his veins. He even had to adjust his position in the driver's seat of the Scout because the thought of seeing Melissa was giving him a hard-on.

At a corner store he picked up a bag of ice. It was too warm outside to want coffee, so he made a pitcher of iced coffee instead. Made sure that the sugar bowl was full. Straightened the magazines in the waiting area. Cleaned off his desk. Checked his telephone messages.

"Hi, Mr. O'Malley," her recorded voice sounded loud in the room. "This is Melissa. I'm really sorry to do this to you on such short notice, but apparently I caught some type of bug and I'm going home sick today, so I've got to cancel our appointment." Her voice did sound a little off, he admitted. "So I guess I'll see you on Friday." A beep, then the message was over.

Devlin dropped down into the chair behind his desk. He was deflated. All that excitement about seeing her again, then this. If he had known on Saturday, he might have—no, he chastised himself, he would still have stayed away from her and the immigrant center. They both needed at least a day to process what had happened during Friday night's session. But damn if this wasn't hard to take. He hoped she was okay. He hoped she really was sick. She could be too uncomfortable to face him. But if that were true, he reasoned, she wouldn't have added the line about seeing him again. So he had to believe that she was telling the truth.

He got through the next day with Mac's company and the help of the Red Sox. It was opening day at Fenway Park and the two of them always went together, had been going since they were old enough to pay for their own tickets, and with the exception of that spring thirteen years ago, they hadn't missed a game since. Mac had V.I.P. seats now, thanks to one of his club members, but it didn't matter where you sat at Fenway. Opening day was still opening day. The excitement of a new season rippled through the stands. When the team ran out onto the field in their crisp white uniforms, everyone stood. When Neil Diamond's voice singing Sweet Caroline filtered through the sound system during the seventh inning stretch, everyone sang. The smells of hot dogs, beer and sunscreen filled the air. Watching the fans alternately cheering and booing as the game progressed was half the fun. Whether the team won or lost, Devlin always went home happy. Today the Red Sox won.

Thursday was as normal a day as he was likely to have, and Friday was more of the same. He got through them, did what he had to do, and when he locked the office up after the last regular appointment he went straight to the club. Anything to prevent himself from watching the clock every five minutes until it was time to see Melissa again.

Friday afternoons were notoriously slow for business. From Memorial Day to Labor Day the club wasn't even open then, but this Friday the lack of people suited Devlin's mood. He ran on the treadmill, did some bench and leg presses, and finally relaxed in the jacuzzi, if what he did could be called relaxing.

There was a fire in his veins that could only be quenched in one way; by one woman.

She looked dressed for bed in a soft cotton t-shirt and drawstring flannel pants. Her nose was a little red, her eyes a little bloodshot, and he was pleased to see this evidence that she had, indeed, been suffering from a spring cold and not avoiding him.

"Hello, Melissa," he greeted, not rising from his chair because even in that loose, casual outfit she turned him on and he didn't want her to see the evidence of that.

"Hello," she returned, shutting the door behind her.

"Feeling better?" he asked.

"Yes. Thanks."

"Glad to hear it. Now let's talk before we get started," he said seriously, making sure that he had her complete attention.

"Okay," she agreed, though her voice and face reflected her uncertainty as she took a seat across from him.

"I missed seeing you this week," he commented.

Blue eyes looked back at him, but she said nothing.

"You have come a long way in a short time, Melissa," he remarked.

"Thank you."

It had been an observation, not a compliment, but he understood.

"How are you feeling?" he asked.

"Better. I took Tuesday and Wednesday off, but then I went back to work."

Devlin smiled at her response. "No, I meant, how are you *feeling*?"

"Oh!" She blushed and shook her head. "Good," then elaborated, "Really good."

"I'm glad. And you slept well?"

"Yes. I used the candle each night. It helps a lot."

"Excellent. Then I think you're ready for what I have planned."

"What's that?" she asked nervously.

"The full monty."

"I don't understand," she confessed.

"I'm sorry. I should have given you a direct answer to your question."

Devlin came around to sit in the chair beside her. Taking her by the shoulders, turning her gently toward him so that they were face to face and there could be no mistaking what he had to say. "I'm talking about sex, Melissa."

She swallowed hard. "Tonight?" Devlin nodded. "Here?" When

he nodded again, her breathing increased its pace and her right hand nervously tucked her hair behind her ear.

Devlin kissed her on the forehead, squeezed her shoulders reassuringly. "Ready?"

She trembled, squared her shoulders, and whispered, "As ready as I'll ever be."

When they went into the therapy room, she looked from the wooden bench to the unopened sofa bed with confusion. "Where should I go?"

"Why don't you go into the bathroom and get comfortable while we wait for the surrogate to arrive," Devlin suggested.

"What do you mean, comfortable?"

Devlin looked at her anxious face, her wide blue eyes, and came to take her hands in his. They were cold. He buffed them between his own to warm them.

"You can leave your shirt and socks on if you want," he told her. "But you'll need to take the rest off."

If possible, her eyes widened even more.

"The light won't be on. Just the candle. No one will see you."

"Just you."

Devlin shook his head in the negative. "Not tonight," he explained.

She trembled, her breathing going shallow.

"Shh," he said soothingly. "I'll be in the office. I just won't be in the room."

"Why not?" she asked, the beginnings of panic in her voice.

Because I'll kill the surrogate if I have to watch him bring you any more pleasure than last week, he thought, but said, "I don't usually stay in the room with my clients, Melissa."

"But you have been," she argued.

"True," he admitted, "but that was foreplay. This is different."

She entreated him with her eyes, her mouth working anxiously, but he said nothing. Just waited.

"I don't know if I can do this," she finally admitted.

"I think you're ready," he told her. "You were fine last week."

"That's because you were there."

"I can't always be there, Melissa."

She looked away, as if ashamed by her admission. At length she said, "It's your voice, you see."

When he said nothing, she continued, "Your voice makes me feel safe. I don't think I'll feel safe without it."

Devlin sighed raggedly. As much as he would love to help her out, he couldn't. Not only would it be a bad idea, professionally, because she needed to be able to have sex without him present, but it would be a bad idea, personally, because he felt way too much for this woman to watch her with another man again. Last Friday's orgasms had threatened his very sanity. As much as he couldn't wait to see her tonight, it was the woman he wanted to see, not a carnal show with her in the leading role.

"Please?" she whispered, her heart in her pleading blue eyes.

Calling himself a fool, he replied, "Okay, but just for the first few minutes."

She smiled with relief and disappeared into the bathroom, leaving him to light the candle and turn off the overhead light. When she came out, wearing the t-shirt and stockings, she went directly to the wooden bench, slid into place and waited.

Devlin got on behind her as he had done the previous week, adjusting their positions until the grooves were lined up comfortably against her inner thighs. Then he reached around her body and took her hands in his own. They were no longer cold.

Stroking her right palm, he said, "Tonight there is no key." She tensed a little at the reminder. "Instead you are free to walk away whenever you want to. You do not need a key. All you have to do is tell me if you want to stop. Just call my name. Okay?"

She nodded, remembered the darkness, and said, "Okay."

"Good girl," Devlin whispered. He kissed the top of her head, inhaled the scent of her, and reluctantly slid off the bench so that the surrogate could take his place. Forced himself to step back. To watch while the other man got into position behind her.

With his mouth the surrogate nuzzled the nape of her neck, rolling his face against it until her hair parted and his tongue found her left earlobe. The long piece of jewelry that she wore dangled there and he sucked it into his mouth. At the same time he used his hands to raise her own and slide them beneath her t-shirt, up her torso, stopping only when her breasts were cupped in her palms then closing her fingers around them. With his thumb he flicked the nipples until they were puckered and hard.

"You take over for him," Devlin instructed. "That's it," he soothed, as the surrogate released her breasts into her care and removed his hands from beneath the shirt only to take it by the hem and slowly roll it up her body.

"What?" she asked, halting her own movements.

"Shh," Devlin whispered. "Keep going. I'll let you know when your help is needed."

The other man took the shirt off one sleeve at a time so that she would not stop completely. When it had cleared her head he dropped it on the floor beside them and brought his hands back to cover her own, squeezing slightly to reassure her.

"Are you watching the light, Melissa?" Devlin asked.

"I forgot," she confessed.

"You have to keep your eyes on it if you're going to relax. And I need you relaxed."

"But I wasn't relaxed last week," she objected, her voice faltering and trailing off as she realized what she had said.

"That's right. But I need you to relax at the beginning. That way I'll know that any tension is natural."

"Okay."

"So I want you to look into the light. Watch the candle flicker. Play with your nipples for me. Make them hard and pointed so they'll be ready for my mouth when I'm ready to swallow them."

As soon as the words cleared his lips, Devlin bolted from the room. He caught a glimpse of the surrogate's shocked expression, but he couldn't blame the man. They had worked together enough to have a system in place and it did not involve anything as personal as what Devlin had just said to Melissa. He was losing it. Just like Mac said he was.

Out in the office he paced from one end of the room to the other. It didn't help. He could still see her in his mind, with her breasts bared in the candlelight. Could still feel her in his memory, her lithe body warm and relaxed. Could still hear her, crying out during her orgasm.

"Mr. O'Malley!"

Devlin squeezed his eyes shut and leaned his head against the windowpane. He swore he could hear her as if he was in the room.

"Mr. O'Malley! I want to stop!"

Chapter 18

Separation

He was in the treatment room between one breath and the next. Melissa, still on the bench, had her hands over her breasts not to play with them but to shield them from view and her body was bowed in on itself. Her blonde hair hung forward so he couldn't see her expression, but he could hear the soft cries coming from her and they weren't cries of ecstasy. Meanwhile the surrogate stood several feet from her, hands held high to show that he was no threat. Devlin spoke quietly to the man, walked him to the front door, then locked it before returning to his client.

She was still exactly as he had left her. Devlin scooped up her t-shirt, placed it in her hands, and sat on the bench beside her.

"Are you okay?" he asked with concern.

"I'm sorry," came her muffled reply.

"You have nothing to be sorry for, Melissa. You just weren't ready for this."

She pulled on her t-shirt and turned to face him, her cheeks wet in the light from the candle.

"But I was," she disagreed.

Devlin smiled wryly. "I hate to argue with you on that, but you did ask to stop."

"That's because you weren't here. I was afraid without you."

Taking a deep breath, Devlin considered his response. He had been worried about his own growing attachment to her because he knew it was unhealthy. In the meantime she had been forming her own unhealthy attachment to him. He had told her in the beginning that he wouldn't pull any punches, though, so he decided to just give it to her straight.

"I'm afraid I can't help you, Melissa."

"What? Yes, you can! You have already!"

He smiled sadly, the movement pulling his damaged face and hurting him on the outside while inside he was hurting at what must be done.

"If I helped you at all, it was because you were ready. Just like dieters. You know, they go on diet after diet but none of them work, then suddenly they find one that does. It's not because the diet is magic; it's because they're ready to commit to one and follow it through."

He saw her throat work as she swallowed, digesting his words.

"It's more than that," she whispered after a long pause.

"It is," he admitted, "but not the way you're thinking."

"What do you mean?"

"I can't help you because you've become dependent on me."

She was silent. It was true and they both knew it, but he couldn't leave her thinking that she was to blame.

"And I've become too fond of you," he added at last.

They had an appointment scheduled for Tuesday in his office to formally end their relationship and debrief the events of the Friday night sessions, the last one in particular, but Melissa didn't show. She didn't call. Devlin wasn't surprised. He told himself that he wasn't disappointed, either, but it was a lie. And while it was easy to lie to himself, he couldn't keep anything from Mac.

"What are you hiding?" Mac asked as soon as their dinner arrived on Thursday night.

"I'm not hiding anything," Devlin denied automatically, hating the other man's perceptiveness. He was supposed to be the one who read people.

"Try again," Mac countered, putting his fork down.

So they were going to get serious about it, Devlin thought, pushing his own plate forward and reaching for the glass of iced water to the left of it. Giving himself time. Mac simply watched him, waiting.

"I let Melissa go," he said at length, voice hoarse, unrecogniz-able. He cleared his throat and looked away from the other man. Mac had blue eyes. Devlin didn't know when he would be able to look into blue eyes again and not see Melissa.

"It was the right thing to do," Mac said quietly.

Devlin knew that. He realized he had been on the verge of jeop-ardizing his career, the one thing he had that made him get out of bed in the morning. If he had continued as her therapist he would have ruined both their lives, hers by confusing her even more than she already was about men and sex, his by crossing a line that no psychologist should ever cross and guaranteeing himself an audi-ence before the ethics review board.

Telling himself that he had done the right thing didn't make it any easier. He was alone again. Would always be alone. Sure, he had Mac but eventually his best friend was going to marry and have half a dozen kids and Devlin would still be that orphan with no ties to anyone. The kid who had been thrown away by one parent and neglected by the other.

Most of the time he could look at his life unemotionally, with the clinical detachment that made him so good at his job, but he didn't want to be detached from life. Always looking on while other people loved together, cried together, lived. He didn't want to be that boy who had to accept what he was given, good or bad, because he had no choice.

He had loved Masha. There was no doubt about it in his mind and no one would ever convince him otherwise. She was smart, and spirited, and argumentative. Perfect for him. He didn't want refined or sophisticated. Didn't want mellow. Devlin wanted to *feel* and with her he had. Then she was snatched away from him and he had spent the last thirteen years in an emotional vacuum.

Until Lexie recommended him to one of her customers at the pharmacy.

How was he to know that in the space of a few weeks his world would be turned upside down again? Where he used to search for a skinny girl with long brown hair and heavy brows, he now longed to see a tall, thin blond woman. One who was quiet, and slightly stubborn, and made him feel again for the first time in thirteen years. But for her own good he had sent her away.

"Dev?" his best friend interjected and he realized that it probably wasn't the first time his name had been called.

"Yeah," he answered, picking up his fork, pulling his plate toward him, "I'm here."

Three weeks later Devlin returned to the immigrant center for the first time since he stopped seeing Melissa as a client. Otto had called to let him know there were some forms requiring his signature, and Reba promised to fatten him up with good Jamaican food if he arrived at noon. It was also that time of the month when they celebrated anyone among them having taken the oath of citizenship.

So he timed his arrival for midday and found the cafeteria full. American flags served as centerpieces on each of the long tables and red, white and blue banners hung from the corners of the ceiling. A CD of John Philip Sousa music played in the background. A head table festooned with patriotic ribbons was set before the windows that looked out on the playground and holding a place of honor behind it were Mr. Chey, his wife, and their first daughter.

Devlin congratulated the three of them. Mr. Chey tried to tell him about the ceremony the day before, but his wife and daughter kept talking over him, speaking rapidly in a combination of English and Cambodian, sounding angry even though they weren't, so eventually the beleaguered man just smiled and raised both hands, giving up.

Devlin took an empty seat at the nearest table. Reba fussed over him, making sure that he had a large glass of punch decorated in Jamaican style. She apologized for the lack of rum and hurried away to get some of her special salad, knowing that he had a fondness for the grilled dish full of pork, fruit and spices.

He was just digging into the meal when a clamor at the Chey table drew his and everyone else's attention. Mr. Chey was beaming from ear to ear, the women were standing on either side of him, gesturing and prattling on, and in the middle of it all was a tall, thin woman with blonde hair. Devlin sucked in his breath and held it.

"Your Melissa, she make coconut chicken curry for them," Reba explained from where she stood over him, making sure that he was enjoying her dish. "She been practicing for this. Look like she got it right."

Devlin couldn't take his eyes off her. The slim gracefulness of her movements as she served bowls to each member of the Chey family. Those pale, slender hands that he had held, that he had warmed. The soft blonde hair that fell just to the tops of her shoulder blades. Hair that she didn't like to have touched. But he had touched it.

He waited for her to turn and notice him. *'Turn around,'* he said in his mind, the words becoming a litany, because he needed to see those high cheekbones, the finely arched brows, the bright blue eyes. Needed to see that she was alright. Needed to see her reaction to him being there.

Was she sorry for not coming in that Tuesday, sorry that she hadn't called? Had she moved on already and found another therapist, or had she regressed and sworn off men forever? Did she think of him? Had she missed him as much as he missed her? Or had the attraction between them all been just a figment of his desperate imagination?

She laughed at something Mr. Chey said, the curve of her cheek rosy, then she was turning to leave. Turning toward him. Her mouth went slack. Blue eyes went wide. Her feet stopped moving.

For a moment they were both suspended like that, eyes locked across the few feet that separated them, and Devlin knew that if he didn't cross that distance he would be sorry for the rest of his life. Rising slowly from his seat he bridged the gap between them.

"Hello, Melissa," he greeted quietly, unable to resist taking one of her slim, blue-veined hands in his own.

"Mr. O'Malley," she breathed, swallowed, gathered her composure. "I didn't expect to see you here."

Devlin smiled sadly. Was she surprised or disappointed?

"I always come to the citizenship celebrations."

"Oh."

Was this to be it, then, he wondered. He couldn't let it be. "How have you been?"

She shrugged her shoulders slightly, took back her hand and used it to tuck the hair behind her left ear, revealing a single piece of jewelry in the image of a U.S. flag.

"Cute," he remarked on seeing it.

"Oh!" She smiled a little self-consciously. "I couldn't resist."

"No reason to." He was watching her face, but he hadn't missed the outfit she had on. A long navy skirt with a red and white striped sailor shirt. "You look very patriotic," he remarked.

Silence fell between them. Where did they go from here, he wondered? They weren't friends, though he liked her very much. They weren't lovers, though he probably knew her as intimately as anyone else did. By his choice, they were no longer doctor and client. Here he was the relationship expert and he didn't know what to say or how to act with her.

It was Melissa who closed the distance between them. Not physically, as he had done when he got up from the table, but figuratively.

"Can I see you again?" she whispered.

Devlin swallowed, afraid. "How do you mean?" he asked.

"Not in the office. Not as your client," she spelled out, blue eyes full of entreaty.

"What did you have in mind?" His voice was a guttural throb. His throat was raw with emotion.

"A date?" she suggested, her eyes darting away from him as soon as the suggestion passed her lips.

Devlin's whole body exhaled. "I'd like that."

They met on Monday afternoon at Boston Common. Holding hands, they joined a group of people following an 18th century costumed guide along the Freedom Trail, a two and a half mile red line walk through the historic city. They admired the King's Chapel grave of the first woman to step off the Mayflower, were suitably awed by the number of stories the patriots had to climb to hang the lanterns in The Old North Church to warn that the British were coming, and they basked in the spring sunshine while standing at the Bunker Hill

Monument. As important as each of the sixteen stops on the tour were, none of them compared to being in Melissa's company. Devlin spent more time admiring the curve of her cheek, the arch of her eyebrows, the smile that fleetingly crossed her face when she forgot to be self-conscious. Like when she stopped to look at a flower arrangement in someone's window box. "I love these," she enthused, fingering the orange and yellow blossoms amidst the vined green leaves.

Devlin spent an hour online that night looking for those plants. When he had finally identified them as nasturtiums, he found someone to deliver a pot of them to her at work the next day. She called as soon as she got them. Unfortunately, he was with a client at the time so he didn't hear the message until the end of the day, but it was worth the wait.

"Hi, Mr., I mean, Devlin," she stuttered, and he realized that she had not called him by his first name before. "This is Melissa. I'm just calling to say thank you." Her voice trailed off and he thought the message was over until she added softly, "I've never had flowers before."

Devlin leaned back in his chair and closed his eyes. A smile pulled at his scarred face. He realized he was happy, because she was happy, because he had done something for her that no one had ever done before. Something he had never done for anyone else. In all his life he had never had a woman to send flowers to; not a mother, a sister, a steady girlfriend. Melissa was a first for him as much as he was a first for her.

On Wednesday afternoon he picked her up at the hospital after lunch and they drove down to the Cape. Devlin had told her to dress casually and bring insect repellent with her. So she was wearing a practical pair of shoes, long pants, and a shirt with sleeves that ended at her elbows. He knew that her modesty had something to do with the choices, but he was glad to see that she was practical all the same.

They went first to Mashpee so that he could show her the camp. He explained about his summers there. They walked the trail between Mashpee and Wakeby Ponds, laughing at the fish jumping for bread crumbs Devlin had packed for that purpose.

"I like it here," she said, looking out over the water from the peninsula knoll that they stood on. "I can see why you liked coming here as a kid."

"It was my escape," he admitted.

"You're lucky you had one."

Devlin came to stand behind her. Tentatively he placed his hands on her shoulders and was rewarded when she leaned back against him, putting her palms over his fingers.

"What about you, Melissa?" he asked, resting his cheek against her own. "Did you have an escape as a child?"

She tensed for a moment, then relaxed and laughed softly. "The kitchen."

"Even then?"

"I was a chubby little girl."

"I find that hard to believe," he chuckled.

"Oh, believe me. It's a good thing I'm tall or you might have been rolling me out here to see this."

Devlin smiled at the image.

"Is that a hint that you're hungry?" he asked after a minute.

Melissa turned in his hold, her hands settling lightly at his waist. "I'm hungry," she admitted, but her fevered expression telegraphed a message that was not about food.

Cautiously Devlin moved his hands down from her shoulders to the small of her back and stepped closer to her. "I don't want to scare you off," he found himself admitting.

"Please," she whispered. "Please kiss me."

He folded her gently against him and softly brushed her lips with his own. She moved into the embrace, wrapped her arms around his middle. "Again," she encouraged.

This time he kissed her as he had been wanting to. Not as a psychologist but as a man. Not with a client but with a woman. He angled his head to the side and claimed her mouth as an equal.

She learned quickly. Where her response was amateur at first, it soon developed into an eager exploration of his mouth. Her hands gripped the back of his shirt and she leaned deeper into him.

Her stomach chose that moment to growl loudly.

They broke apart, laughing. Devlin clasped her hand in his, gave her one last kiss on the lips and said, "You really are hungry after all."

So they walked back to the Scout and drove to a clam shack where they indulged in stuffed quahogs followed by blackened swordfish before heading back to the city. Devlin was pleased when Melissa reached out in the darkness of the Scout's interior to rest her hand against his thigh. He would have liked having her up against his side, but the vehicle was a standard so he had to settle for just that contact until they arrived in the hospital parking lot where she had left her car.

He turned off the ignition and reached for her. After just one small hesitation, she came easily into his arms. "I like being with you," he husked, kissing her soundly and showing her with his body how much he meant it.

"Me, too," she breathed a moment later. "With you, I mean."

"When can I see you again?"

"Tomorrow night?" she suggested, her voice holding a note of eagerness that did wonders for his ego.

"I can't," he said ruefully, and for once he really was sorry that he and Mac had a standing Thursday dinner date. "How about Friday?"

"Friday is good," she agreed.

"Where would you like to go?"

There was a moment of silence and he felt her brace herself before suggesting, "I'd like you to come to my place."

Now it was Devlin who stilled. It was dark in the interior and he didn't want to interpret her invitation in the wrong way.

"For dinner?" he asked.

"For dinner," she confirmed, and he felt her head bob against his shoulder. "But not just for dinner."

"Melissa," he cautioned. Afraid that she was moving too fast for her own good. Afraid of his own reaction.

"Please," she said, her voice sure. "I want this. I want to be a whole woman. With you."

"I don't want to hurt you," he admitted, knowing that there was a very real chance he could.

"You'll hurt me if you don't say yes," she told him.

Devlin leaned his head against the seat rest. He was too far gone to tell right from wrong, but he knew what felt good, what felt right, and that was being with her.

"Okay," he agreed at last.

She surprised him by leaning over and kissing him soundly on the lips. "Good. And, Devlin?"

"Yes?" he asked, surprised by the timid note in her voice after such a demonstration of confidence.

"Can you bring the bench with you?"

Chapter 19

Explosions

He left the bench in the Scout while they had dinner. Melissa had really put on a spread for him, with lobster bisque, tossed salad and char-broiled steak. He noticed that although she loved her food, her portions were not large. Or maybe that was because she, like him, was too busy thinking about what would follow their meal to actually enjoy it.

When their small talk had petered away to nothing and the food was going cold on their plates, he made the first move.

"Why don't I go downstairs for the bench while you get more comfortable?" he asked, noting her denim overalls and long sleeved shirt.

Her exhaled breath was one of relief. "Yes, that sounds good."

Devlin reached over and gave her hand a reassuring squeeze before coming to his feet and stepping outside into the hall. He went down the stairs and out to the Scout, grabbed the bench and his duffel bag, and came back into the building but didn't immediately go to her apartment. He wanted to give her a few minutes to get ready. To be sure she was ready. Or to back out.

He knew that wasn't going to be the case when she answered his knock on the apartment door. She was dressed in a loose t-shirt that barely covered her thighs, her feet were bare, her hair was down, and through the open doorway behind her he could see a candle flickering against the wall. Her face bore a look of determination that would have made him laugh under any other circumstances.

Instead he gave her a reassuring kiss before advancing into that shadowed room.

Devlin barely noted the double bed against one wall. His attention was on the center of the room and the bench in his hand. He was eager to put the furniture down, eager to set it up and guide her down onto it. This time there would be no surrogate between them.

She slid onto the bench first, aligning her inner thighs with the smooth grooves created for that purpose. The t-shirt rode up against her flesh and almost, but not quite, bared her to his sight. Devlin's pulse raced as he slid into place behind her. He still had his clothes on because he wasn't sure how she would feel about his naked flesh against her, but the pants he wore were tear-away athletic pants in a silky material and his t-shirt could come off at any time.

"Are you ready, Melissa?" he asked her now.

"Ready," she said, voice definite.

Devlin leaned forward and nuzzled the nape of her neck. Blew against her skin and gloried in the shiver that action brought. He did it again. Her hair parted and his tongue found her left earlobe, sucking it and the jewelry there into his mouth. Chills erupted along her body. He could feel them. Feel her legs clench around the seat to contain them.

Going slowly, he slid his hands beneath the loose t-shirt, up the soft flesh of her abdomen, and cupped her breasts.

"I can't wait to get my mouth on these," he whispered, flicking the nipples, enjoying the way they puckered in response. "Do you remember me telling you how I wanted to swallow them, Melissa?"

She squirmed on the bench in front of him and her breath came out in little pants.

"Do you like it when I talk to you that way, Melissa?"

She was silent for a moment before admitting, "I don't know. I think so." He felt her shrug before adding, "It makes me feel funny."

Devlin smiled, pleased with her response.

"Hmm," he murmured, bringing one hand up the center of her back until it gripped the nape of her neck and running the other one down to rest on her inner thigh. "And this?" he asked, laving the jeweled ear with his tongue. "How does this make you feel?"

She shuddered and gasped. "I can't hold still when you do

that."

"Interesting," he said, for once using a pat psychologist's phrase, but only because he was getting turned on too and his ability to speak coherently was fast disappearing.

He had to mentally brake himself, though. Make sure this was what she wanted.

He decided to test her readiness by sliding his hand up from her nape into her hair, tugging lightly until her head was turned slightly and he had better access to her ear. She didn't resist at all. One more fear, a top fear, conquered. He had touched her hair. Devlin was proud of her for that and grazed her temple with his lips.

He brought her head back to rest against his shoulder, her neck arched and exposed, and bit softly at the tendons there. "Are your nipples ready for me?" he asked.

She squirmed against him and a tremor ran down her spine.

"Melissa?" he pushed, the hand in her hair tightening the smallest bit and the one at her thigh doing the same.

"Yes," she gasped.

"Yes, what?"

"Yes, they're ready for you." Then, in case he wanted more, "My nipples are ready for you."

"Good. I'm hungry and I plan to make a feast out of them," he warned her.

Feast on them he did. With her body pulled back against his own and angled off to the side, he latched onto one breast and immediately pulled the whole thing into his mouth. He tortured the tip with his tongue while his cheeks bellowed in and out as he suckled. When she thrust it deeper into his mouth, straining against him, he reminded her of what she was supposed to be doing, returning her now lax hand to the other breast. She played with it for a few minutes, readied it for him, and only then did he switch sides.

"Play with yourself," he instructed as he blew on the nipple.

"Where?" she asked.

"Your clit. Play with it," he clarified.

Uncertainly, jerkily, she moved her hands down to the soft delta at the top of her thighs. With one she spread her lips and with the other, found the tiny bud of sensitive flesh there and started to rub.

"Good," he told her. "Have you been playing with yourself since you stopped coming to the office?"

She stilled against him.

"If you stop, I'll stop," he admonished. "Just look into the light. Stroke yourself." He bit her nipple lightly and she jumped. "Now tell me the truth. Did you masturbate these weeks without me?"

"Yes," she whispered, obviously worried about her answer.

"That's good," he told her. "I want you to be able to bring yourself pleasure."

"It wasn't as good as, you know," she faltered.

"When I'm helping?" he asked, moving his hand to play with her free breast while the other one stroked her hair.

"Yes."

"That's normal," he reassured her. "If we could do everything ourselves, we would never mate."

"True," she concurred.

"But I'm here now. No reason to do everything for yourself when you don't have to."

With that, he dropped the hand at her breast to join her own hand at the core of her body. He applied pressure to the back of her palm, adding force to her circles. She undulated back against him and tossed her head on his shoulder.

"That's it," he praised, lowering his left hand from her hair to the breast on that side and lightly plucking at her nipple.

She ground back against him in response.

"Keep going," he said.

Her breathing started to escalate. Her hand sawed frantically at her clit, reaching. She switched angles, tried harder. He pinched her nipple, then rolled it between his thumb and forefinger at the same time that he removed his other hand.

"Don't force it," he admonished. "If you're going to come, you'll come."

"I can't get there," she breathed, upset.

"Shh," he soothed. "You're still a beginner. Practice makes perfect, and you haven't had much practice. Slow your strokes down."

She did as he told her to. He slid his hand down the inside of her thigh and found her cunt, slipping a finger inside at the same time that he rolled her turgid nipple.

"Ride my finger," he told her.

She stilled her motions, uncertain.

"Don't get nervous now, Melissa. You're doing fine. But I want you to ride me."

He grabbed her earlobe with his mouth, rolled her nipple with his hand, and pumped the finger on his other hand in and out of her. She rocked back and forth, easily finding the rhythm for her ride. Her buttocks bumped against his erection. Her pelvis thrust down and back.

Devlin added another finger, then pushed her hand out of the way to use his thumb for stimulation against her clit.

"Play with the nipple in my hand," he instructed, waiting until she had taken over for him, then arching her back so that he could take the other one into his mouth. He licked it, bit lightly, then suckled it into his mouth and swirled his tongue around the pebbled peak.

Melissa came at once.

He let her ride the storm to its conclusion, pulsing against his finger, buffeted against his body as he kissed and petted her on her way down until she lay limply against him, breathing hard.

When she recovered, he eased her up into a sitting position and slid both of his hands into her hair. His fingers raked over her scalp. His thumbs feathered over the base of her skull while he scraped lightly against the sides of it, above the ears, tilting her head slightly forward until the nape of her neck was exposed for his mouth.

He sipped at the tender skin there. Beginning at the hairline, he made his way down the ridge of her spine until he reached the middle of her back, slowly pressing her forward as he did so.

"Grab the sides of the bench with your hands," he instructed. When she had complied, he pressed her further toward the surface and followed her down, continuing with his oral ministrations. He ran his feet up the front of her legs and nudged them backward. Then he brought his hands down, ran them the length of her arms to the wrists, and removed them from where they grasped the wood to place them over pegs on either side of the bench above her head. He kissed the center of her back between her shoulder blades and blanketed her body with his own, stretching over her so that he could reach the front legs of the device. With a small lift they unhinged and he folded them up under the top, then gradually lowered the front of the bench to the floor, at an incline, pressing the top of her body down with it.

Devlin ran his hands back up the length of her arms then down her sides to her breasts, hanging over the edge of the bench on either side where it was narrowed. He kissed her back, toyed with her breasts, and caressed her shins with his feet.

"Are you okay?" he questioned softly.

"Uh-huh," Melissa answered, her voice slurred a little in the aftermath of her orgasm. "But I don't think I can lift my head to see the candle from here."

"Do you need to see it?"

"No. As long as you've got my back, I know I'm safe."

"Oh, I've got your back alright," he said, licking the length of her spine until he reached the nape, then laving it in a return journey, all the way to the base of it where her buttocks plumped out to protect it from harm.

Melissa squirmed and giggled. "That tickles," she complained.

So Devlin did it again. And she giggled again.

He eased away from her then, keeping his hands at her sides so that she knew he was there even as he lifted his chest away from her back and came upright. Then he pressed close against her, thigh to thigh, while he reached over the side of the bench and extracted a condom from his pants on the floor. He tore the foil wrap open with his teeth, pulled the prophylactic out, and rolled it onto his waiting cock. Discarding the packet, he slid one hand beneath her belly to find her still wet. Ready for him. Lifting her hips slightly away from the table and increasing the angle at which she was bent, he entered her from behind.

A ragged sigh escaped her lips.

Devlin kept his movements slow at first. Then he added a hand at her clit so that each time he surged forward, his fingers pressed back until she was reaching for them, rocking her backside against him, pushing her pelvis toward the wooden surface, using her feet on the floor to gain leverage, to increase friction. Devlin dropped down over her, grabbed her hands over the pegs that she gripped, and rode her.

They were both panting, both rushing for the same conclusion. She twisted her right hand out from beneath his and brought it beneath her body, working her clit. Smart girl. He brought his right hand up and raked the leather gauntlet on his wrist against the tender flesh of her nipple.

"Oh my god," she wailed, back arching and buttocks slamming into his belly. He gripped her nipple and she let go like a breaking dam. Her body shuddered against his, tremors following her all the way down to the bench until she finally rested there, perspiration filming her spine and her hair a mess around her damp face in the glow of the candle.

Devlin wasn't finished with her yet. He hoisted her up by the hips, braced his feet against the floor, and pumped in and out of her soft body until he, too, was shuddering, teeth clenched, neck thrown back in ecstasy. His climax seemed to go on forever, but eventually his shaking legs lowered the rest of him back down to the seat of the bench and his heart rate slowed.

He could barely hear over the blood thundering in his ears, so he didn't notice at first the sounds coming from Melissa, but when he did recognize them, he wasn't surprised. A lot of people cried after orgasms. Especially if it was their first time, or if having one meant release from emotional baggage they had been carrying.

Petting her back lightly, he slid along the bench until he was no longer inside her, then threw a leg over the side to sit and dress.

"Melissa," he said softly. "Can I get you anything?"

"No," came the muffled reply.

"This is pretty normal," he reassured her. "Just let it go. Next time it will be easier for you and you probably —"

"Next time?" she gasped, pulling herself up to a sitting position and hurrying off the bench. "There won't be a next time!" she vowed.

Devlin didn't normally hear this from his clients. He certainly didn't want to hear this from his girlfriend.

"Why would you say that?" he asked. "Are you hurt?"

"No."

"Was it bad?"

"No!" she almost screeched, then dissolved into sobs as she rummaged through a drawer on the other side of the room. "It isn't that," she cried.

"Then what is it?"

"It's him."

"What do you mean?"

"I can't do this again. I just can't. It makes me think of him, and I—I can't."

Chapter 20

Awakening

He could see her outlined in the glow from the candle now and watched her body language. She was dressed but holding herself tightly around the waist like a person who thought they might fall apart at any minute.

"I'm sorry," she whispered for what must have been the tenth time. "I'm so sorry. I thought I could do this, but I can't."

Devlin wanted to point out that she had done it, but he knew that wouldn't help. She was obviously reliving the experience from her adolescence and couldn't separate sex with him from the rape that she had suffered.

"What has you so upset, Melissa? Is it that he took you against your will? Held you against your will? Or is it something else?" Devlin asked quietly, hoping to calm her with his tone and the reasonableness of his questions.

She tried to speak, gulped, turned away and tried again. Finally, in a voice raw with pain, she cried, "He left me!"

"What?" Devlin asked, knowing that he heard her correctly but still disbelieving.

"He left me! I was alone in the world, alone without him, and I couldn't find him anywhere!"

"You tried?" he asked incredulously.

"I've done nothing else since then," she sobbed. "Every time I see a man with a shaved head, with tattooed biceps, I think it's him. I look for him everywhere."

Devlin went still for a moment. But it couldn't be; Melissa had blue eyes. Masha's eyes were hazel. Melissa was born in Maryland

and had no discernible accent. Masha was from a city in Ukraine and spoke like a foreigner. Lots of men in the last couple decades had shaved heads and tattoos.

"Are you looking for this man, Melissa, or are you afraid that he'll show up?" His voice was level, which was amazing considering how he felt. They had just had what he considered mind-blowing sex and she was crying because her thoughts were with someone else.

She moved away from the candle, further into the shadows of the room, and when she spoke her voice was a ragged whisper. "I look for him."

"Even though he abused you?"

"Yes."

"And what would you say if you found him? Have you thought that maybe he has moved on? Or, worse, that he's just replaced you with someone else, has chained someone else to his bed and his side?"

"He wouldn't do that," she denied, her voice full of fierce conviction.

Devlin couldn't believe what he was hearing. He had thought that they were making progress when she was his client, but her feelings for her abductor and rapist were much more complicated than he had first suspected. On top of that, he had been falling for her, obviously deluded into thinking that her feelings for him were growing at the same time and in the same way. The rational part of his mind knew that she wasn't in control of her emotions, but the man in him wanted to rage against this turn of events.

"Melissa," he said slowly, "you do understand that this isn't healthy, don't you? That you have reacted to the fear and helplessness you experienced by imagining this guy as something more than what he really is. It's not unusual in kidnap situations."

"He's not like that," she argued.

Devlin had heard enough. He flipped on the overhead light and put the bench legs back in place so he could carry it down to the Scout.

"You need help, Melissa, but I don't know if anyone can help you," he said, preparing to leave.

"What?" she asked, turning toward him.

"I can't help you. I want more from you than a therapist client relationship. You know that. But I can't even have that, because you're still thinking about him. You have to be ready for therapy to work, and it's obvious to me that you aren't ready to move on and put this man in your past. Where he belongs."

She closed the distance between them and took his wrist, her blue-veined fingers wrapped around the leather cuff he wore as if that grip could prevent him from going.

"How can I?" she whispered, fiercely blinking back the tears that clouded her eyes.

"How can you not?" he returned, putting the bench down on the floor and taking her by the shoulders. She didn't even flinch at the contact and that evidence of progress didn't escape his notice. She was in her bedroom, half dressed, talking to him. When they first met she wouldn't even take off her coat.

"I can't live without him, don't you see?" Melissa pleaded, rubbing furiously at the moisture that rolled freely down her cheeks.

"You call that living?" he demanded. He knew he should remain calm, but he was hurting too.

"I lost my contact!" she shouted.

"To hell with your contact!" he shouted back, giving her thin frame a shake. "Listen to yourself. Jesus, woman, this guy really did a number on you if you still think, after all this time, that you're in love with him."

Her head fell forward and her body sagged in on itself.

"Melissa," he spoke more gently now, "I'm not trying to hurt you. I just want you to see that this John guy is not—"

"Mick," she interrupted.

"What?" he asked.

"His name isn't John. His name is Mick."

Everything inside Devlin went still. From the other room he could hear the ticking of a clock, the breeze playing with a set of window blinds, but inside the bedroom there was not a sound.

Slowly he loosed his hold on her shoulders and slid his hands up to her jaw, using his thumbs to nudge her chin up. Her eyes remained downcast, though.

"Melissa," he said, his voice a croak, amazed that he could say anything at all since he was pretty sure he had stopped breathing, "Look at me."

She shook her head no.

"This is important, Melissa. I have always tried to be patient with you, respected your wishes in terms of how much you were willing to share. Now I want you to respect mine."

"Why?" she asked, in the smallest of voices.

Devlin braced himself. A cold sweat actually broke out across his brow. This could be the biggest moment of his life and it could also be the biggest heartbreak he had ever experienced. To think for even a moment that he had found her.

He realized that he hadn't responded to her question.

"Please look at me, Melissa," he urged.

"What difference would it make?"

"I need to see your eyes."

"No."

"I need to see if one is blue and the other is hazel."

Now she stilled. "Why would you think that?" she asked, her guard up.

There was only one answer he could give, only one word that he could form; a name, one he had rarely uttered for the past thirteen years unless his silent cry every morning and every night could be counted as such.

He gathered her close against him despite her stiff resistance. Wrapping his arms around her, nuzzling the top of her head, he let it go, "Masha."

She leaped away from him.

Literally, she was next to him one moment and two feet back in the next. Her eyes, wide and tear-drenched, were now glued to his face as her own face bleached of all color. One of her eyes was blue; the other was hazel. Beneath them her cheekbones stood out in stark relief and he could see by the movement of her chest that she was laboring for breath.

He understood. Right at this moment he was having a hard time breathing himself. It felt like he had taken a strong punch to the solar plexus and the pain was so intense that he might never recover from it.

"Who are you?" she demanded.

Devlin didn't answer. He could see her inspecting him now, trying to figure out if the man before her could possibly be the same one she had known thirteen years ago. It was hard to tell, since he had a full head of hair now, his face was scarred, his body bulkier. Even his voice had changed as a result of the accident and age. So he did the only thing he knew of to answer her question. Keeping his movements slow, he drew the hem of his shirt up over his head and revealed his arms to her. ad servire and et tueri. To serve and protect.

Melissa fainted.

Chapter 21

Revelation

She came to as he was moving her from the floor where she had crumpled to her bed. "This can't be happening," she moaned.

"Shh," he whispered, cradling her against his side then easing her down onto the mattress. "It will be all right."

She lay back against the pillow and stared up at him with her one blue eye and one hazel eye. In that face he could now see the two women he had loved in his life. Yes, loved, if he admitted it now. Despite his resistance he had been falling in love with Melissa for some time. She just hadn't resembled Masha enough for him to see that the woman was what became of the child.

The brown hair was gone, dyed blonde he supposed. The eyebrows had been plucked. She was several inches taller than at sixteen and her body had filled out, now lean instead of skinny. She spoke English without an accent. With contacts her eyes were blue.

Those eyes filled with tears and her lower lip trembled. He started to reach for her, but she put her hand up to ward him off, at the same time scooting up against the headboard.

"I need a drink," she said.

"Okay," Devlin smiled, thinking he could use one himself. "What can I get you?"

"Just water," she replied.

"Coming right up."

He was glad of something to do. Moving into the kitchen he found the light, then the glasses, but the last thing he expected when he returned to the bedroom with the water was for her to pull a gun on him. The drawer in the nightstand was open, so she must have taken it from there. In her other hand was a pair of padded restraints like he had used on her ankle during their earlier sessions.

"Put these on your right hand and the bedpost," she said, tossing them across the comforter in his direction. "Slowly."

Devlin knew that he could probably disarm her in a heartbeat. He was quick and smart. But he didn't want to hurt her ever again and that included taking control away from her, so he grabbed the links, snapped one around his hand and the other around the tall bedpost at the foot of the bed.

"Now what?" he asked.

For answer, she picked up the telephone on the nightstand, dialed the star key and two numbers, and waited for someone to answer the call. When a male voice sounded over the receiver, she looked him squarely in the eye and said, "I am calling for Ryan MacGilvary. My name is Masha Wozny. I need your help."

Devlin's eyes widened. He thought she was calling the cops. Maybe some thugs to beat him up. Certainly not Mac. He listened as she gave Mac her address and disconnected the call.

For half an hour they stared at one another. Devlin stood loosely at the post, trying to look unthreatening while his eyes devoured her.

She removed her blue contact, put it in a case on the nightstand, and pulled her hair back into a ponytail. The dangling jewelry in her left earlobe winked at him and he recognized it for what it was; a guitar pick. She had often worn one of his in her ear thirteen years ago. A lump rose in his throat at the sight of it.

When the knock came at the door, she called out, "In here, Mr. MacGilvary," and a moment later Mac entered the room.

"What is going on?" he demanded at seeing the gun in her hand and Devlin secured to the bedpost.

Melissa had gasped and paled at seeing the other man, who she recognized from the restaurant. The gun faltered in her grasp, then dropped with a soft thud to the carpeted floor. Her hazel eyes, wide as saucers, were fixed on Devlin's face. "It *is* you," she whispered.

"It's me, baby," he confirmed, his own eyes moist with thirteen years of loneliness and longing for this woman.

"I don't believe it," Mac breathed, and Devlin saw a look of horror cross his best friend's face as his gaze swung from one of them to the other. "It can't be."

"Yes, brother, it can," Devlin said wryly. "Ryan MacGilvary, I'd like you to meet my Masha."

Mac was speechless for a moment, still looking back and forth between the two of them, but then he slid his cell phone out of his pocket and punched in some numbers before saying, "I am going to need you in here after all."

A few seconds later Lexie came into the room. She didn't see Melissa at first, because of where Mac was standing, but she spotted Devlin right away with his hand cuffed to the bedpost. "This is definitely better than sleeping at home in my own bed," she breathed. "Can I take a picture?"

"Lexie," Mac scolded, sweeping his arm out to indicate the woman on the bed.

"Melissa?" the big girl asked. "But—" she turned to Mac, her face puzzled, "I thought you said you got a call from dickhead's lost love. Marcia something or other."

"I am Masha," Melissa stated clearly.

Three sets of eyes turned to look at her now. Devlin's with yearning, Lexie's with rounded surprise, and Mac with uncertainty.

"I am Masha Wozny and I am also Melissa and I'd like you all to leave now."

Mac took Lexie's elbow and started leading her from the room.

"Take your friend with you," Melissa added.

If Mac was uncertain before, now he was downright baffled, but he was a gentleman so he extended his hand for the key that Melissa offered and reached up to set Devlin free. As soon as he had, Devlin was on the bed and reaching for the woman there.

"Get away from me!" she shrieked, her voice panicked, jumping off the other side. "I want you to go!"

She was crying again, harsh sobs that wracked her body as she wrapped her arms around her middle and backed away from him.

"But Melissa. Masha. It's me, Mick," he said.

She turned to Mac, saying only a simple, "Please."

"Time to go, brother," his best friend said solemnly. Devlin looked between him and Melissa. If he approached her again, she probably would call the police this time. He couldn't read her emotions, couldn't tell what she was feeling except that she was upset, but he could read Mac clearly enough and knew he had taken on the role of protector. He would do whatever he had to do for her in that moment.

"I'll call you," Devlin said with defeat as he headed for the door.

She wouldn't take his calls. Wouldn't see him when he showed up at the hospital. Wouldn't admit him to her apartment building when he tried to see her there. For two weeks he had no contact with the one person in the world that meant more to him than life itself.

"What do I do?" he asked Mac over his third J&B on the rocks at his apartment two Fridays later. "How do I get through to her?"

"Dev, I wish I knew what to say," Mac admitted. "I've never heard of anything this unreal outside of television before."

"I don't know if she's not seeing me because she's afraid to or if she's just trying to figure it all out."

"I couldn't tell you. Lexie tried calling her, but Melissa said she didn't want to talk right now."

"She's all alone, Mac."

"I know."

"If she's trying to figure it out, she has no one to help her. No one to even talk to about it. She can't exactly tell people that she's got a fake name and past and, by the way, her rapist's henchman is now her therapist and how should she handle that?"

"They'd probably lock her up."

"Yeah," Devlin groaned, raking his hands down his face, scratching the puckered skin of his scars and drawing blood.

"Now you're a mess," Mac commented. "Or more of a mess, I should say."

"I just don't know what to do."

"It will come to you, brother. You always know how to get through to people."

The next morning Devlin woke with a hangover, but he also woke with a purpose. He called the immigrant center to see if she was still meeting with Mr. Chey. Reba said that she had missed a date two weeks ago, but was there the week before and expected again to-day. Devlin ended the call, satisfied. Then he called Lexie, much as it pained him, and after promising on his life that he would not come to the pharmacy, asked if Melissa was still making her Sunday night trips there. She played with him for a while, telling him that she had a degree and what made him think she would still be working at that job, then eventually relented to say that yes, Melissa still came every Sunday night, but sometimes she was earlier than she used to be. Next he called Sergeant Webster's widow to see if she could direct him to anyone with international experience. She didn't know, but said that her son might; he was a captain in the police department now. So he called that man and, trading on his relationship with the father, got information from the son to help him in his quest.

He was busy all week getting ready. He didn't call Melissa. Didn't try to visit her. Didn't even talk to others about her. When Mac asked how he was doing, he told him honestly that he was do-ing well. When his best friend looked at him skeptically, Devlin just smiled and told him not to worry, that he had a plan.

On Sunday he rented a four-door sedan from an auto dealer. It was dark blue, ordinary, non-descript. Unlike the mottled relic he usually drove that everyone recognized from a mile away, he could travel in this car and draw little attention. He was counting on it.

He hadn't lied to Lexie when he said he wouldn't come to the pharmacy. But he also hadn't told the whole truth because when Sunday evening rolled around he was in the pharmacy parking lot in the rented sedan. On the seat beside him he had everything he would need to execute his plan. There was nothing else to do but wait.

Melissa arrived at about twenty minutes to closing. Since it was a balmy night, she had shed her jacket and was dressed in light clothing, though still modest. A simple pullover top and cotton slacks. Her hair was pulled up into a French twist and even from his hiding place behind the steering wheel he could see a silver hoop dangling from her ear. As soon as she entered the store, he backed his car into the spot beside hers, his driver's side next to her own. Then he opened both of his doors on that side and, using them as shields, went to work disabling her automobile by simply removing her front tire and throwing it into his trunk. He put a note on her windshield explaining that she would return for her car in the morning before resuming his vigil in the front seat of his rented sedan.

She came out of the pharmacy a few minutes later, a clutch purse in one hand and plastic bag dangling from the other, her keys firmly in her grasp. Flashing headlights in the car beside him indicated that she had unlocked her doors, and Devlin used the driver's side mirror to time her approach and his move.

Melissa came to a dead stop when he stepped out of his car, which worked to his advantage. Not giving her time to even call for help, he grabbed her around the waist with one arm, yanked open the rear door of his car, and pushed her onto the back seat, following her down to hold her still. She flailed her arms, trying to gain purchase so she could raise her torso and buck him off. He grabbed each of her wrists and held them still until she finally stopped fighting.

"What do you think you're doing?" she demanded.

"I think I'm holding you down in the back seat of this car," he replied with absolutely no apology in his voice.

"I can't believe that you would do this."

"You wouldn't come to me, so I had to do something," he explained patiently.

"Because I don't want to see you!" she screeched, almost unseating him with a hard pelvic thrust.

"Lying to yourself again, Melissa?"

A sound of throttled rage came from the back of her throat.

Devlin took a deep breath. Said the single most important word he had ever uttered. "Please."

Melissa stilled beneath him. "What do you want from me?"

"I just want a little of your time. Honestly. If you still want to leave when I'm done talking, I'll let you go."

She eyed him doubtfully, and he couldn't blame her. After all, he had just abducted her, for all intents and purposes, from the parking lot and was holding her down in the back seat of a nondescript vehicle that didn't belong to him.

That realization shook him and he dropped her hands immediately. Sat up and away from her.

Melissa looked bewildered by his actions. Again he couldn't blame her.

"Just talk," he reiterated. "Okay?"

Eventually, reluctantly, she nodded. Devlin opened the door to let her out but kept hold of her hand while he walked her around to the front seat, just in case she changed her mind. Then he slid behind the wheel and turned the vehicle in the direction of Pleasure Bay.

"Now what?" she asked when they were upstairs in his condo and he had locked the door behind them. She was giving a brave performance, but her voice wavered a little and she looked around nervously, inspecting the room for any hidden threats. When her eyes fell on the guitar hanging on the wall they widened. She swallowed hard and took a step backwards.

"Now you come with me," he replied.

Taking her by the elbow, he led her into his bedroom where there were only three pieces of furniture; a king-sized bed with bookcase headboard, a wall unit large screen television, and a straight backed wooden chair. It was set up to face the television.

"Here you go," he said, leading her toward the seat.

Melissa dug in her heels and would not go any further. "I'm not going in there," she stated.

"Yes," he said with confidence. "You are."

When she continued to balk, he lifted her bodily, keeping her pressed against his side so that her kicking legs could not do any damage, finally managing to sit down on the wooden surface with her on his lap.

"You said you would give me some time," he reminded her.

"I didn't say I'd go into your bedroom."

"Please," he said again, and realized that he had used the word more in this one night than at any other time in his life. "I promise nothing bad is going to happen to you, Melissa. It's just a room. It's just a chair."

"Then why can't we talk in the other room?"

"The television is in here," he explained, nodding toward the wide flat screen covering most of the wall.

"What does that have to do with anything?"

"Just hold on for a minute."

He rose and came to kneel in front of her, face to face. "I'm not going to hurt you, Melissa," he said softly, reaching up to brush her hair back where it had loosened at the sides in their struggle. "I promise." Then, unable to resist, he leaned forward and pulled the silver hoop at her ear into his mouth, lapping at the lobe and nuzzling her with his face.

"Please stop it," she whispered. "I can't handle this."

Her voice was sincere and he recognized the limit he had pushed her to. Easing away slowly, he moved to the headboard where he grabbed a remote control. A second later the television screen beeped on and Melissa was faced with her own image staring back at her. It was just her head and shoulders, but it was live feed and showed her, sitting in his bedroom on the wooden chair.

"What is this?" she asked, a tremor in her voice.

He could see her trembling where she sat. She probably thought he had some kind of kinky punishment planned for her in retaliation for not taking his calls.

"Just keep watching," he soothed.

When he was certain that the picture quality was good and that she was not wearing her contacts so her true eye color was showing, he hit a button on the remote to shrink her image into a small box in the top corner of the screen. The rest of the monitor was taken up with the log-in box for Skype. Devlin advanced to the television, pulled a keyboard out from beneath it, and punched a few keys. He was standing directly in front of it so she could not see what he typed or who was facing him when he asked, "Can you hear me all right?"

"No problem," a man's voice answered.

"And can you see Masha okay?"

Melissa probably found it odd that he would use her Ukrainian name.

"Perfect," the man assured him.

Devlin stepped away from the screen, turned to the side, and watched her face. Saw the confusion as she was confronted by the image of a man she did not know, then curiosity when that man got up out of his seat and two bodies moved before the camera that had captured him. Midsections appeared, a flash of brown hair as someone turned to adjust the seat behind them, then two women sat looking at her. One was in her fifties, one in her twenties, but both of them had light brown hair, hazel eyes, and happy smiles on their tear-drenched faces.

Almost mirror images of the girl he had known thirteen years ago. The same girl who, now a woman, gasped and stared at the screen with disbelief. Then when the older woman cried, "Masha!" the floodgates broke open. Crying, laughing, all talking at the same time in a language still foreign to Devlin, they couldn't say what they had to say fast enough, but they tried. They had thirteen years to catch up on.

Coming to stand beside her, Devlin squeezed Melissa's shoulder, dropped a kiss on top of her head, and left the room.

The reunited Wozny family talked for almost two hours. During that time, Devlin made a call to Lexie to let her know that he had abducted Melissa from the parking lot, just in case it was caught on tape, and to ask that she not call the cops on him. He would have the car picked up tomorrow and if she wanted, he would have Melissa call when she was done with her Skype transmission to confirm that she was safe. The pharmacy clerk turned radiology tech had a few choice words for him but agreed not to do anything, provided she had confirmation that her customer was okay before noon of the next day.

He popped his head in the doorway every few minutes, just to make sure that the connection wasn't faltering, but otherwise he stayed out of the room. He cleaned out his refrigerator. Swept the kitchen floor. Went through some junk mail that had accumulated on the table. Played some chords on his guitar. He was doing that when she called out to him. "I'm all done."

Devlin hung the guitar on the wall and slid the pick into place.

He approached the bedroom cautiously, not sure how Melissa would be dealing with the unexpected and overdue reunion with her mother and younger sister. She sat slumped in the chair, head down, giving him no indication of her emotional state.

"Melissa?" he said softly, coming to stand beside her, his hands loose at his sides, waiting for whatever she needed to do or say.

She surprised him in the best possible way, one moment sitting motionless in the chair and in the next launching herself at him. She clutched him around the waist, pulled him close, buried her head against his side, and sobbed. Not the loud, wracking sobs that he had witnessed from her before, but quiet and cathartic tears of relief that broke Devlin's heart all over again.

Chapter 22
Lost and Found

He held her while the emotional storm raged, then held her some more when it had drained away, leaving her limp against him. Eventually he slid his hands beneath her thighs and carried her to his bed. She made no protest when he undressed her and tucked her in. She said nothing while he shed his own clothing and climbed in beside her. Was silent when he wrapped his arms around her and nestled her head against his shoulder. It was only after the recessed track lighting in the bedroom and the small lights along the headboard were out that she spoke. "Thank you," came the heartfelt whisper.

"Don't ever thank me," he admonished. "You deserve so much more."

They lay quiet for a few minutes until she spoke again. "What is your real name?"

"Devlin."

"Devlin. Not Mick," she said.

"No. That was just an Irish slur. It worked well for undercover."

"I like Devlin," she decided.

"I'm glad."

A pause, then, "Devlin?"

"Yes, Melissa?"

A single sob escaped her and she gripped his torso. "Please don't ever leave me again."

"Never," he vowed fiercely. Rising above her, he took her face in his hands and angling his mouth over her own, kissed the woman he loved. A kiss of longing, of love denied, of promises to come. "Not for anything in the world," he said as tears flowed freely from his own eyes.

"I don't know how to live without you," she admitted. "I tried, but—"

"I know," he said, stopping her words with another kiss. "I know." He rolled onto his side and brought her body against his own, flesh to flesh, front to front for the first time since they had met as Devlin and Melissa. "I was lost without you," he told her. He slid his leg between her thighs and pulled her snugly against him. "So lost."

"What happened to you, after they took me away?"

"I lost it," he admitted.

"Lost it how?"

"Tried to kill myself."

Her gasp was loud in the dark room.

"That was because of me?"

"Don't you see, I had failed you. I was supposed to protect you, but I couldn't find you, couldn't make sure you were okay."

"You tried?"

"Hell, yes, I tried. They told me that I would blow your cover, jeopardize the case. Said your new identity had to be protected if they were ever going to take the organization down and ordered me to stop or they would arrest me. Put me on suspension anyway."

"I can't believe they did that!" she exclaimed, sounding truly angry.

"They were right. I would have kept looking."

She rolled away from him and a moment later the lights above the headboard came back on. Devlin blinked to see her sitting up against the bookcase headboard, her expression furious.

"What is it?" he asked.

"Those bastards," she ground out, and he could see tears in her hazel eyes. This was more than anger.

"Masha?" he asked with real concern, sliding up to sit beside her. He wanted to reach for her but wasn't sure he should. Her arms were crossed in front of her, holding the covers to her chest in a death grip.

"What is it?" he asked again.

Her throat worked a few times before she was finally able to choke out, "They lied to me."

"They did?"

"They told me that you had moved on to another case and that I was nothing but a job to you."

Devlin was silent. Of course they would say that, but only if she had asked about him.

"You were the only person I trusted. I wanted to see you, to have you tell me what was happening. They told me, but I didn't know them. They could have been lying to me just like Kraus did. They were lying to me."

Devlin chose his words with care, trying not to let his anger at the situation creep into his tone. "They did what they thought was best for you. And they were right. I would have blown your cover, put you at risk." He hated to admit it, but it was true.

"No!" Melissa denied fiercely. "You don't understand."

"What don't I understand?"

"They didn't give me a cover."

"What?" Now Devlin was confused.

"I mean, they protected me until the trial. Told me to pick out an American name, something with the same initials as my old name. So I picked Melissa Wright. They sent me to live with a family in Virginia, set me up with a home school program."

"So they did protect you," he remarked.

"But only until the trial. I guess you have to have a judge or something approve the request for protection. It was denied."

"What?" Devlin demanded, a chill running down his spine.

"Yes. They tried again, but it was denied again. I guess I just wasn't that important a witness. If something happened to me, they still had enough evidence to put the ring away."

Fear for her safety rushed over Devlin like an icy wind off the Atlantic. He was speechless with it.

"By the time the trial was over and it was obvious no one cared about me, I had finished the high school course and started college under my fake name. So I just changed it, legally, and kept pretending."

Devlin was still at a loss for words.

"They told me not to get in touch with my mother at first, because she could be in danger, then when the trial was over, I just didn't know what to say to her. I wanted so much to go home, but, but by then I didn't know how I could. I had become this other person."

"Alone," Devlin croaked. The realization that both of them had been alone all this time was breaking his heart. Even worse was the realization that the federal government had decided that she, a victim, was dispensable, and had abandoned her in a way that even he had never done. This precious woman could have been lost to him forever.

"Alone," she agreed, placing her hand against his cheek, the loneliness in her hazel eyes matching his own. "Devlin?" she asked softly.

"Yes, Melissa?"

"Make love to me."

He had been waiting to hear those words pass her lips for thirteen years.

Almost reverently he placed his hands on either side of her face and brought her mouth down to his own. Kissed her with longing, with love. Slipped his fingers into the braid at the back of her head and released her blonde hair from its confines, spreading it out around her shoulders, toying with the ends of it, admiring its softness.

"I have missed you, my Masha," he breathed, burying his face against her neck and inhaling her scent for a long moment. She smelled sweet, and clean and fresh. He nuzzled the side of her neck, her earlobe, skimmed her cheek with his lips before bringing them back to her own.

"Don't hold back," she told him now. When he hesitated, she continued, "I've been waiting all my life for this, Devlin. Don't treat me like a girl. Don't treat me like a client. I want all of you this time."

"Baby, you've got me," Devlin promised, smiling and not caring that one side of his face pulled into a grotesque mask.

He kissed her briefly on the lips but moved away, leaving her bewildered as he made a path with his lips down her throat, over her clavicle bones, before going directly to one nipple. He rolled it once, twice, with his tongue before pulling it into his mouth and suckling on it.

Melissa's stomach muscles contracted and he could hear her gasp of surprise above him. Then she was raking her fingers through the thick darkness of his hair, pulling him closer.

"I'm going to touch you tonight," she whispered against his ear.

Devlin shook at her words. His hands tightened at her waist. When she wrapped her legs around his hips, just as he had taught her to, he slid lower down her body. Used his hands to massage her breasts even as his mouth moved over her abdomen.

She flinched in response. Began to tremble. By the time his mouth reached her inner thigh, her legs were shaking and her hips were coming off the bed in anticipation.

"Not like this," she begged, and Devlin lifted his head, worried that he had misread her reaction, that she was scared instead of aroused.

"What's wrong?" he asked.

"It's not equal," she explained, sitting up.

"What do you mean?"

"I mean, I want us to be equals."

Before he could guess her intent, she swiveled on her hips so that she was lying down facing in the opposite direction, her head near his calves, her hand running up the inside of his thigh. Her eyes gleamed and a pleased smile broke across her face as she said, "You can continue any time you like."

Devlin had a hard time concentrating after that. When she put her hand on him for the first time he almost leapt off the bed. When she wrapped her fist around the base of his cock he thought he would die. Instead he retaliated. Bit softly on the inside of her thigh, then blew on it. The sound that came out of her at that was loud, high, and indistinguishable, but there was no doubt she liked it. He took advantage of her momentary distraction and pressed down on her clitoris with his thumb. She ran her own over the slit of his penis while grasping the root with her fingers and pumping lightly.

"You're killing me," Devlin groaned, his breath warm against her inner thigh, making her flinch.

"We'll both die happy," she murmured, just before the tip of her tongue replaced her finger to lick away the dew that beaded on the head of his cock.

He slid a finger inside her body. Found her warm and ready. She laved the perimeter of his cock with her tongue, pulled the head between her lips. He added another finger, rotated his thumb.

Melissa sucked in her breath, her lips going lax against him for a moment. Then she clamped down hard on him, using her lips like a vice to hold him, surrounding him with a tight, warm, wet cavern.

"I'm in heaven," he breathed, using his thumb to separate the folds of skin protecting her clitoris and pulling the little piece of flesh into his mouth.

"No, no, no, no," she complained, the word garbled because she had her mouth full. Pulling her head back, she let his cock pop free and his body collapsed with disappointment. "That's too good," she objected, half rising on an elbow. He moved his fingers inside her and suckled on her flesh. "Devlin, I can't take that," she whimpered, falling back onto the bed. "You've got to stop."

Smiling down the length of her body into her dazed and feverish eyes, he whispered, "Make me."

She snapped back to full consciousness in a hurry. Stared at him with her mouth agape. Groaned when he plucked at one of her nipples with his spare hand. Flinched when the fingers inside her found an erogenous zone that she hadn't known existed.

"Make me," he growled against her flesh.

She started to ask how, saw his cock bobbing wildly just inches from her face, and finally understood the challenge.

"You may be sorry before you're done," she teased, taking hold of him with both hands. Rolling her cheek against the length of him. Pulling her nipple free of his grasp so that she could turn her torso onto its side and sandwich his cock between both breasts, using them as an anchor to hold him still while she took the tip between her lips and slid the length of him down her throat. He knew that she had never done this before, but she was so good at it she was killing him.

He renewed his efforts to please her. Reached up with his free hand to grasp the nape of her neck and help her find a rhythm. She moved up and down on his flesh like a piston. Laved him with her tongue, gripped him with her gums and dragged her mouth up the length of him until he was almost ready to pop out before plunging down on him again.

Devlin was about to lose his mind. He took the hand from her neck and grasped one of her breasts between his fingers, rolling and pulling on the nipple. It rose to the occasion immediately. Melissa's movements became almost frantic. He grasped the other nipple, quickened the pace with his other hand and pressed down hard with his thumb.

She came apart with a low keening cry. Tried to keep him in her mouth but couldn't as her lower body shook violently and her abdomen convulsed. She tried to talk but had to use all her energy just to breathe.

Devlin waited for her to come down, her body limp, the perspiration that had filmed her now cooling, before he lifted her and settled her back into her original position on the bed. Her blonde hair spread out across the pillow. Her eyes looked drugged. He slid up beside her and placed his hand on her flat stomach.

"Melissa?"

"Hmm?" she murmured drowsily.

"We're not done, you know."

"Not done?" she repeated, then embarrassed, said, "Oh! I wanted to make you feel good, and —"

Her words dried right up when he touched her. Put his fingers against her clitoris and rubbed.

"See?" he prompted.

"But how can that be?" she gasped, her lower body already undulating against him.

"Women can go many times," he assured her.

"And men?"

"Not so many. But I'm good to go if you are."

Her breathing was rapid again, her lassitude completely gone. She reached out and fisted his cock. "Tell me how you like it," she smiled.

"Ride me," he answered at once because she deserved this. If ever any woman deserved to set the pace, she did.

Melissa smiled in anticipation. Removing herself from his grasp, she got onto her knees, then straddled his hips before pausing there. "I'll need your help," she admitted.

He knew that. It was one thing to understand the mechanics of a position but something else to know how it really worked.

Devlin brought her hands down beside his shoulders, then took her hips, guiding her onto him. Once she was comfortable, he helped her to sit up again before showing her how to establish a rhythm.

"You're so brave," he praised her.

"Only because it's you," she admitted. "I could never do this with someone else."

Still so naïve, Devlin realized, if she could make a statement like that and not know what it did to him. How it healed him.

"Bring your breast to me," he told her, waiting while she lowered her upper body over him so that he could pluck it with his lips and pull it into his mouth. When he swirled his tongue around the tip she moaned. When he used his thumb to play with the other nipple, she lost her rhythm. He helped her find it again by sliding his other hand between their bodies and rubbing her clitoris. Automatically she followed his lead, rocking against him in time with his hand.

Devlin thrust up inside her but never stopped his ministrations. She lost her breath. He did it again. She started to shake. He suckled her breast, and rubbed her clitoris, and rolled her nipple.

"It's happening again," she wailed, her hips slamming into his now.

"Good. Bring it on," he told her. "I want all of you this time."

She didn't hold back. Just when she started to shatter, he surged up inside her and his body clenched so hard in ecstasy he thought he broke his back teeth. Above him Melissa was sobbing her release. He gripped her hips to hold her still and pumped into her. Once, twice, three times. His thighs were locked in spasm, buttocks tight, his head thrown back and his eyes tightly closed against the pleasure. He didn't even realize he had held his breath until he finally collapsed down onto the bed and the air came rushing out of him.

Thirteen long years but it had been worth the wait. Unlike their one and only time in the cabin, unlike that night in her apartment, they had made love as equals.

Devlin rolled onto his side and pulled her with him, reaching to the foot of the bed to retrieve the covers. He started to reach for the light switch, then stopped and looked at her.

"What is it?" she asked drowsily.

"I love you, Masha," he said solemnly, "and I love Melissa too."

She opened her mouth to respond, but emotion got the best of her and nothing came out. Her hazel eyes misted over. She swallowed hard.

"Do you love me?" he prompted for her.

She nodded.

Devlin kissed her on the mouth, turned off the light, and settled back against the pillows. She snuggled against his side. Their breathing slowed and they drifted off to sleep in one another's arms.

Devlin woke to a beautiful sight. Masha was sitting astride his naked body, her own naked body exposed for his viewing pleasure, and she was smiling at him. "Masha," he sighed.

"Melissa," she corrected.

"You'll always be my Masha, baby," he told her.

"Good. Let's see if you still feel that way when I'm done with you."

"Huh?" he asked, planning to sit up and only then realizing that his hands had been cuffed to the base of his bed.

"How does it feel?" she purred, coming down low above him until her body was just a breath away from his own, then rising again. "This time it's you who is locked up, but I'm still the one with the key."

"You will always have the key," he told her sincerely.

She put a finger to his lips.

"No talking," she ordered. "Unless you want me to gag you, that is."

They smiled at one another.

"That's better," she nodded, coming down above him again but this time sliding her legs out from around his hips and shimmying low against his body until her elbows came to rest on either side of his thighs and her beautiful face, propped in her hands, was looking at him over the length of his turgid cock.

"Hmm, what have we here?" she teased, eyebrows raised. "I think I'd better check this out."

She extended her tongue, just the very tip of it, and ran it around the purple head in a dainty, cat-like motion.

That's when he heard the condo door open.

"What the—?" he started to ask, trying to rise, but was held firmly in place by the cuffs at his wrists and the woman in his lap, then it was too late.

"Guess we really didn't have anything to worry about after all," Mac said from the doorway to the bedroom, Lexie smirking at his side.

Melissa shrieked in alarm. She jumped up off Devlin, realized she had just bared his genitals to their audience, grabbed the side of the sheet and covered him, then realized that she was nude before them and took it back to cover herself. Finally she gave up, pulled the material over her head, and collapsed onto Devlin's chest.

Mac laughed.

"I really like this woman," Lexie said. "Her taste in men might suck, but at least she knows how to treat them." She nodded to Devlin's bound arms. "Anyone who is smart enough to tie you down before messing with you is all right in my book."

"Bitch," Devlin retorted.

"You two are going to be the death of me," Mac sighed. "But I can see we're superfluous to the situation here. Anything you need before we go, brother?"

"No." Devlin smiled from ear to ear, a rare thing since he met this woman thirteen years ago. He didn't even care that the expression disfigured his face, and neither did Mac, who smiled in return. "Just shut the door on your way out."

"Got it," Mac nodded, taking the elbow of the woman at his side. "Let's go, Lexie."

"Oh, Mac?" Devlin called just as his friend was reaching for the doorknob behind him.

"Yeah?"

"I'll expect you to be best man at the wedding."
Now it was Mac who smiled from ear to ear.

He and Mac went out that weekend to celebrate one last time together. It was Melissa's idea. She had noticed that when they met to go over the wedding arrangements with those who would have a role in them, Devlin's brother stood apart. Alone. Everyone else seemed to have someone but not him. The man who took care of those he loved, no matter what they needed, had no one to call his own. Devlin ordered two draft beers from the bartender, paid for them, and walked over to where Mac was sitting at a corner table.

"Hey, brother," Mac said as he accepted one of the glasses.

"Talk to me," Devlin said.

"About what?" Mac asked with surprise. "It's your night out. And shouldn't you be with your bride instead of me?"

"She told me to come out. Make sure you're all right."

"She did?" Mac raised his eyebrows. "That was thoughtful of her."

"Yes, it was."

They drank together, held their glasses at their chests, watched as the news flickered over a television screen above the bar.

"I'll always be here for you," Devlin said. "You're my brother and marriage doesn't change that."

"Of course it will change," Mac denied.

"Not when it comes to what's important."

Mac shrugged.

"I hate to see you alone, brother," Devlin finally said, revealing his thoughts and revealing Mac's insecurities at the same time.

"Don't worry about me," his best friend said, turning now to face Devlin, a gleam in his eyes and a smile on his face. "I've got my next project all mapped out."

"You do?" Devlin asked, curious.

"Remember? I told you that it wasn't about profit this time, that I had to wait until certain things were taken care of before I could make my move?"

"Yeah," Devlin recalled.

"Well, you're all taken care of," Mac said, slapping him on the back, grinning, "and I hope she's ready, because this is going to be one special takeover. So don't you worry about me; you've got a bride to keep you busy."

They wed at the club just two weeks later on a Friday night. Fridays would always be their night. Melissa couldn't have a big wedding because with a false identity she had no family to invite and, although she could probably resume her real name at this point, everyone knew her as Melissa.

Mr. Chey walked her down the red carpet that served as an aisle. She wore a simple white dress that complemented her lean silhouette and carried a bouquet of purple lilacs that she handed off to Lexie who stood waiting with Devlin and Mac. Reba threw rice at her even though it wasn't time to. Sergeant Webster's widow beamed at him as if he was her own child. Gremlin had set up a recorder on a tripod and was using a camera to snap shots of the ceremony.

They wrote and read their own vows.

"Devlin, I don't know why I love you," Melissa began, and their guests laughed. "I only know that I am not me without you. When we are old, and our children are grown, I will die with you because there is no life for me without you. But until that time comes, I will love you every single day that we have together."

Devlin looked into the most beautiful face he had ever seen, the hazel eyes that he so loved, and a lump rose in his throat.

"Melissa," he said, his voice gravelly with emotion so that he had to clear it before continuing. "I don't know why I love you. If someone were to ask me, I would not have one single thing that I could point to as the reason. All I know is that there is no me without you and no joy in this world when you're not with me. You hold my heart. You are my heart."

Otto Faust, acting in his role as justice of the peace, then asked the appropriate questions and they gave the appropriate answers.

Circlets of gold were exchanged.

"Time for a dance," Genie announced from where she stood to the right of them, and Devlin gladly took his woman in his arms. "This number was personally selected by the couple to represent how they feel about one another."

Genie was a performer. He/she had a beautiful voice so when it came time to a wedding song, Devlin could think of no one to do it better. Her mellow sound filled the room while he and Melissa swayed softly to the music, clinging to one another.

> *"There you are in the early light of day.*
> *There you are in the quiet words I pray."*

Devlin held her closer, knowing that he would cherish every single moment they had together. The boy who came from nothing, had nothing, finally had someone of his own.

> *"Every time I take a breath,*
> *And when I forget to breathe."*

Devlin thought that if he ever lost her again, he would stop breathing for good. Thirteen years of emptiness lay behind them. A lifetime, however short or long it ended up being, stretched out ahead of them. One spent together.

> *"There you are the earth and I'm the moon."*

Like the moon, he would always be drawn to this woman, would always circle around her, would always be grounded by her.

We do our best to proof all our work, but if you spot a text error we missed, please let us know via our website Contact Form at http://forbiddenfiction.com/contact.

About the Author

Ann Ruby lives in rural New England where the winters are long and dark, just perfect for reading, writing and romance—not quite the three Rs discussed in her day job as an academic. When she isn't immersed in some kind of print, she likes to spend time outside enjoying the clean waters and scented forests that surround her home.

Works by Ann Ruby:

Blindsided
Covert Passion

About the Publisher

ForbiddenFiction.com is a publisher devoted to writing that breaks the boundaries of original erotic fiction. Our stories combine intense sexuality with quality writing. Stories at Forbidden Fiction.com not only arouse readers through sensations, but also engage them emotionally and mentally through storytelling as well-crafted as the sex is hot.

ForbiddenFiction.com is also designed to be a social reading environment. You'll have fun even if just reading the latest post each day, yet you will have the chance for so much more. Readers and authors can be part of ongoing discussions of specific works and individual authors as well as more general topics.

Sign up for a FREE Membership today at ForbiddenFiction.com